語用為綱國際漢語教學系列教材

Book 1

CANTONESE
in Communication:
Listening and Speaking

邊學邊用
粵語聽說教材(一)

總主編　吳偉平

編　審　李兆麟

商務印書館

Cantonese in Communication: Listening and Speaking [Book 1]

Series editor: Weiping Wu
Editor：Siu-lun LEE
Reviewer: The Yale-China Chinese Language Center of the Chinese University of Hong Kong
Executive Editor: Elma Zou
Cover Designer: Mobing Li

Published by
The Commercial Press (H.K.) Ltd.
8/F, Eastern Central Plaza, 3 Yiu Hing Road, Shau Kei Wan, Hong Kong
http://www.commercialpress.com.hk

Distributed by
SUP Publishing Logistics (H.K.) Ltd.
3/F, C & C Building, 36 Ting Lai Road, Tai Po, N.T., Hong Kong

Printed by
Elegance Printing & Book Binding Co., Ltd.
Block A, 4/F, Hoi Bun Industrial Building, 6 Wing Yip Street, Kwun Tong, Kowloon, Hong Kong

First Edition and second printed in December 2019
©2018 by The Commercial Press (H.K.) Ltd.
ISBN 978 962 07 0512 0
Printed in Hong Kong

邊學邊用：粵語聽説教材（一）

總　主　編：吳偉平

編　　審：李兆麟

審　　訂：香港中文大學雅禮中國語文研習所

責任編輯：鄒淑樺

封面設計：李莫冰

出　　版：商務印書館 (香港) 有限公司

　　　　　香港筲箕灣耀興道 3 號東滙廣場 8 樓

　　　　　http://www.commercialpress.com.hk

發　　行：香港聯合書刊物流有限公司

　　　　　香港新界大埔汀麗路 36 號中華商務印刷大廈 3 字樓

印　　刷：美雅印刷製本有限公司

　　　　　九龍觀塘榮業街 6 號海濱工業大廈 4 樓 A

版　　次：2019 年 12 月第 1 版第 2 次印刷

　　　　　©2018 商務印書館 (香港) 有限公司

　　　　　ISBN 978 962 07 0512 0

　　　　　Printed in Hong Kong

Table of Contents

LESSON 1

Introducing yourself　介紹自己

LESSON 2

Asking and indicating the way
問路指路

LESSON 3

Going out to have fun   出去玩下

LESSON 4

Going out and shopping　行街買嘢

LESSON 7

Seeking advice from medical doctor
約見醫生

LESSON
8

Talking about holidays   傾下假期

LESSON 9

Traveling and touring in Hong Kong
暢遊香港

LESSON 10

Saying goodbye and farewell
講聲再見

GENERAL REVIEW L1-L10

Appendices　附錄

PREFACE

The Yale-China Chinese Language Center (CLC), founded in 1963, became part of the Chinese University of Hong Kong (CUHK) and has been responsible for teaching Chinese as a Second Language (CSL) to university students in the past decades. In 2004, we launched the Teaching Materials Project (TMP) to meet the needs of students in different programs. Over the years, the hallmark of all TMP products is the use of the Pragmatic Framework, which reflects findings from research in sociolinguistics and their applications in CSL.

Compared with the two published series designed for learners with background in Chinese languages and cultures (*Putonghua for Cantonese Speakers* and *Cantonese for Putonghua Speakers*), the current series, designed for non-Chinese learners [*Chinese (Putonghua) in Communication* and *Cantonese in Communication*], has moved further in making pragmatic factors an integrated part of CSL teaching materials. Some of the salient features common to the series are highlighted below, while characteristics in each volume and guide to use the textbook are explained in the INTRODUCTION following this PREFACE.

Guiding principle: Language learning is a process that includes four key stages based on the counter-clockwise approach in CSL learning (assessment, curriculum design, teaching materials, teaching and teacher training), all of which ideally should follow the same guiding principle. Using a textbook designed with theories in structuralism for a curriculum with a communicative approach, for example, will lead to confusion and frustrations for both teachers and learners. The compilation of this series follows the same principle that guides the other three key stages in CSL teaching and learning as practiced at CLC, which treats contextual factors as part of the learning process.

Aims: By using this textbook with the matching learning and teaching strategies, it is expected that communication in Chinese by learners will be not only correct linguistically, but appropriate culturally. It is also expected that, with the focus on using while learning, the speaking proficiency of the learner will improve in both quality and quantity (from sentence to paragraph to discourse).

Authenticity (from oral to oral): Teaching materials for speaking Chinese, to the best extent possible, should come from spoken Chinese. Instead of "writing the texts according to the lists of vocabulary and grammatical points", a common practice in almost all teaching materials preparation, we have pioneered the approach that starts from spoken data and, based on authentic spoken data, works out a list of vocabulary for active use, grammatical points and pragmatic points. This challenging approach, dubbed "from oral to oral", is believed to bring learners closer to the authenticity of spoken Chinese in oral communication.

Pragmatic factors: Attempts have been made to turn pragmatic knowledge in communication from oblivious to obvious, as indicated by the summary table at the beginning of each lesson, which includes information related to participants, setting and timing (or purpose) of the communication event. A limited number of "pragmatic points" are also listed together with "grammatical points" to draw the awareness of learners, and to serve as an indication of the importance to learning such points.

Style and register of spoken Chinese (*Yuti*): Since culturally appropriateness is regarded as a major goal of learning, it becomes an unavoidable task to show the differences in style and register of the language used. Efforts have been made to illustrate the characteristics of style and register in communication for different purposes in different settings, including the choice of vocabulary, grammatical and discourse structure, as well as formulaic patterns. More information in this area can be found in the INTRODUCTION for volume three of this series.

In today's world, it is paradoxical that there are actually far too many textbooks in the CSL field and, at the same time, far too few that can be used as it is when it comes to specific programs and teaching methodology. The following notes are therefore provided to put the current series in perspective:

1. They are designed to meet the changing needs of CSL learners, most of whom are now motivated by the desire to use the language they learn in real life communication.

2. Each of the three volumes in the series can be used for one semester (6 hours per week for 12-14 weeks). For programs with a longer duration, supplementary materials

will be needed.

3. The focus of this series is on the learner's ability in speaking and listening, which will establish a solid foundation for further study that may focus on all the four skills including reading and writing.

As the Director of CLC, it's my privilege to launch this project more than a decade ago with support from the University, to serve as the TMP leader and series editor and to see it become one of the four major academic projects of the Center. I am pleased to see yet one more product from this Project, which will not only meet the immediate needs of our own students, but also serve the CSL community for the sustainable development of the field.

Weiping M. Wu, Ph.D.
TMP Leader and CSL Series Editor
Director of the Chinese Language Center
The Chinese University of Hong Kong
Shatin, Hong Kong SAR

INTRODUCTION

"Cantonese in Communication" is a series of textbooks designed for learners learning Cantonese as a second language. This series of textbooks is suitable to use in programmes designed for university students and working professionals who want to learn practical Cantonese and to use Cantonese in their daily life as well as in their professional life. This book series focuses on spoken Cantonese used in Hong Kong. All examples and sample conversations demonstrated in this series are drawn from authentic speaking materials collected from native Hong Kong speakers. This book series wishes to help learners to increase their Cantonese proficiency with accurate pronunciation and use of linguistic forms in real life situations. This whole series emphasizes on appropriate use of Cantonese and prioritizes the use of language to finish different communication tasks in real world situations. This series tries to put "contexts" and "linguistic functions" together in the lesson texts, as well as in most examples and exercises to train learners to use the linguistic forms learnt in actual communications.

This book series targets to use daily language scenarios, useful vocabulary, lively conversations and exercises to train learners with no Chinese background to be able to use Cantonese in a practical way. This book series uses Yale-romanization system to transcribe Cantonese. This book series has the following characteristics:

Emphasizing contexts and language functions

Providing a variety of exercise for practicing speaking and listening skills

Focusing on practical use of Cantonese

Setting clear stage goals to improve oral proficiency

As the editor of this book, I would sincerely wish this book provides guidance and valuable assistance to Cantonese second language learners. Wish all Cantonese learners would enjoy their learning journey.

How to use the book

This book is a beginners' book targeted to use daily language scenarios, useful vocabulary, lively conversations and exercises to train learners with no Chinese background to be able to use Cantonese in a practical way. This book consists of 10 lessons and 2 general review lessons. The 10 lessons include language scenarios happened in daily life and cover various language functions, such as querying, inviting people, describing, recommending, explaining and expressing thanks, etc. Each lesson consists of the following 7 parts:

1.   CONTEXTS AND LINGUISTIC FUNCTIONS   語境特徵與語言功能

Each lesson of this book states clearly the language contexts and the core linguistic functions presented in the lesson texts and in notes on pragmatic knowledge. This set a goal of what learners can do by using Cantonese after finishing each lesson. The whole book contains different language contexts appearing in real life.

2.   TEXTS   課文

All the lesson texts in this book are based on real life topics and situations. All texts used in this book are adopted from authentic speaking materials taken from native Cantonese speakers in Hong Kong. The lesson texts consist of sample conversations and dialogues. Cantonese characters and Yale-romanization are presented in the lesson for learners to follow. All the texts are also written in Standard Written Chinese and attached in the appendix for reference.

3.   VOCABULARY IN USE   活用詞彙

Each lesson presents vocabulary items which are frequently used when in each language contexts. All vocabulary items are presented with Yale-Romanization, Cantonese characters, part of speech and English translation for learners and teachers to use. All vocabulary items are listed in the appendix for easy reference.

4. **NOTES ON LANGUAGE STRUCTURE** 語言結構知識

This book provides a step-by-step guide on language structure. Each lesson presents syntactic structures and patterns that relate to the language contexts of the lesson. A systematic pronunciation guide is provided from Lesson 1 to Lesson 5.

5. **NOTES ON PRAGMATIC KNOWLEDGE** 語用知識注解

Pragmatic use is the major concern of this book. Each lesson provides pragmatic notes relate to the language contexts, linguistic functions and syntactic structures and thorough discussions and examples are given in each lesson.

6. **CONTEXTUALIZED SPEAKING PRACTICE** 情境說話練習

There are contextualized speaking practices in each lesson to provide an assessment on each stage. Learners can work on the exercises to reinforce what they have learnt and at the same time check what aspects need further assistance.

7. **LISTENING AND SPEAKING** 聽說練習

Reinforcement is important in language learning. In view of this, each lesson provides extended texts or speaking samples for learners to reinforce and consolidate their language skills.

Apart from the 10 core lessons, there are 2 review lessons to provide training and consolidation of learners' language skills. The first review lesson is placed after Lesson 5 and it reviews knowledge and skills presented in the first 5 lessons. The second review lesson is located after Lesson 10 and it is a general revision of all knowledge and skills presented in this book.

Acknowledgement

I would like to express my gratitude to the many people who saw me through this book; to all those who provided support, talked things over, read, wrote, offered comments, and assisted in the editing, proofreading and design.

I would like to express my very great appreciation to the Director of Yale-China Chinese Language Centre, Dr. Weiping Wu, enabling me to publish this book. Dr. Wu provided valuable theoretical inspirations throughout the whole process of this publication. I would also like to thank Ms. Hsiaomi Chu and Dr. Ho-put Wong for their professional supports and continuous encouragement in the making of this book.

I would like to offer my special thanks to Dr. Chunling Xie, Mr. Tianxiao Wang helping me in the process of editing and proofreading. Thanks to Commercial Press (Hong Kong)' ssupports and assistance on the printing and publishing stage. I am particularly grateful for the assistance given by Mr. Yongbo Mao of Commercial Press (Hong Kong) for his long-lasting supports and encouragement.

Last and not least, I beg forgiveness of all those who have been with me over the course of the years and whose names I have failed to mention.

Siu-lun, LEE, (Dr.)
Head of the Cantonese Programme Division, CLC, CUHK.
Editor of *Cantonese in Communication, Book 1*

Abbreviations and Symbols

Adj.	....	Adjective
Adv.	....	Adverb
Att.	....	Attributive
AV	....	Auxiliary Verb
BF	....	Bound Form
CV	....	Co-Verb
DW	....	Directional Word
IE	....	Idiomatic Expressions
lit.	....	literally
M	....	Measure
MA	....	Movable Adverb
N	....	Noun
Nu	....	Number
P	....	Particle
Patt	....	Sentence Pattern
PH	....	Phrase
PN	....	Pronoun
PW	....	Place Word
Q/A	....	Question & Answer
QW	....	Question Word
RV	....	Resultative Verb
RVE	....	Resultative Verb Ending
S	....	Subject
SP	....	Specifier
T Sp	....	Time Spent
TW	....	Time Word
V	....	Verb
VO	....	Verb-Object Compound
/	....	or
( )	....	word(s) that can be left out

Lesson 1 Introducing yourself
介紹自己

1. Contexts and linguistic functions
語境特徵與語言功能 *yúhgíng dahkjīng yúh yúhyìhn gūngnàhng*

Contexts (who, where, when) 語境特徵（人地時）	Linguistic functions 語言功能
Who: new acquaintance **Where:** school, casual gathering, office, etc **When:** first encounter	**Core functions:** Introducing (informal) 介紹（非正式）
Language Scenarios: First meeting, introduce yourself 初次見面、自我介紹	**Supplementary functions:** Greetings 打招呼

Notes on pragmatic knowledge	Notes on language structures

I. How to greet people with similar status
    1. Greeting expressions
    2. Chinese names
II. Related Knowledge
    1. Omission of pronoun in Chinese
    2. Starting questions with "chíngmahn"
    3. Saying "thank you" in Cantonese:
       "ṁgōi" verses "dōjeh"
	- Descriptive sentences
	    Subject-Verb-Object sentences
	- Negative sentences
	- Questions forms
	    ma-type questions
	    Choice-type questions
	    àh-type questions
	- Sentences withyáuh
	- Number Measure – Noun structure
	    (Nu-M-N)
	- Cantonese numbers (1-10)

2. Texts

課文 fomàhn

2.1 In the classroom

老師：	你好！	**Lóuhsī:**	Néih hóu!	
大衛：	你好！	**Daaihwaih:**	Néih hóu!	
老師：	你叫乜嘢名呀？	**Lóuhsī:**	Néih giu mātyéh méng a?	
大衛：	我叫大衛。	**Daaihwaih:**	Ngóh giu Daaihwaih.	
老師：	你好，大衛。 我係李老師。	**Lóuhsī:**	Néih hóu, Daaihwaih. Ngóh haih Léih lóuhsī.	
大衛：	李老師，你好！	**Daaihwaih:**	Léih lóuhsī, néih hóu!	
老師：	大家好，我姓李， 係你地老師。	**Lóuhsī:**	Daaihgā hóu, ngóh sing Léih, haih néihdeih lóuhsī.	
學生：	李老師，你好。	**Hohksāang:**	Léih lóuhsī, néih hóu.	

2.2 On campus

子安：	你好！我叫林子安。	**Jíōn:**	Néih hóu! Ngóh giu Làhm Jíōn.
大衛：	你好！我叫大衛。	**Daaihwaih:**	Néih hóu! Ngóh giu Daaihwaih.
子安：	大衛，你係唔係美國人呀？	**Jíōn:**	Daaihwaih, néih haih m̀haih Méihgwok yàhn a?
大衛：	我係美國華僑，你呢？	**Daaihwaih:**	Ngóh haih Méihgwok wàhkìuh, néih nē?
子安：	我係香港人。	**Jíōn:**	Ngóh haih Hēunggóng yàhn.
大衛：	你係唔係中文大學學生呀？	**Daaihwaih:**	Néih haih m̀haih Jūngmàhn Daaihhohk hohksāang a?

子安:	係，我係中文大學學生。	**Jíōn:**	haih, ngóh haih Jūngmàhn Daaihhohk hohksāang.
大衛:	你係中文大學學生嗄？！	**Daaihwaih:**	Néih haih Jūngmàhn Daaihhohk hohksāang àh?！
子安:	係呀。你呢？	**Jíōn:**	Haih a. néih nē?
大衛:	我都係中文大學學生，中文大學好大。	**Daaihwaih:**	Ngóh dōu haih Jūngmàhn Daaihhohk hohksāang. Jūngmàhn Daaihhohk hóu daaih.
子安:	係呀！中文大學好大，好靚！大衛，你學乜嘢呀？	**Jíōn:**	Haih a! Jūngmàhn Daaihhohk hóu daaih, hóu leng! Daaihwaih, néih hohk mātyéh a?
大衛:	我學中文，我學廣東話，我鍾意中文。你呢？	**Daaihwaih:**	Ngóh hohk Jūngmàhn, ngóh hohk Gwóngdūngwá, ngóh jūngyi Jūngmàhn. Néih nē?
子安:	我學英文。	**Jíōn:**	Ngóh hohk Yīngmàhn.

2.3　In the classroom

大衛:	早晨，呢個係唔係廣東話班呀？	**Daaihwaih:**	Jóusàhn, nīgo haih m̀haih Gwóngdūngwá bāan a?
老師:	係呀。	**Lóuhsī:**	Haih a.
大衛:	你係唔係老師呀？	**Daaihwaih:**	Néih haih m̀haih Lóuhsī a?
老師:	係呀，我係廣東話老師，我姓李。	**Lóuhsī:**	Haih a, ngóh haih Gwóngdūngwá lóusī, ngóh sing Léih.
大衛:	李老師，你好！	**Daaihwaih:**	Léih lóuhsī, néih hóu!
老師:	你叫乜嘢名呀？	**Lóuhsī:**	Néih giu mātyéh méng a?
大衛:	我叫 David White。	**Daaihwaih:**	Ngóh giu David White.

老師：	你有冇中文名呀？	**Lóuhsī:**	Néih yáuh móuh Jūngmàhn méng a?
大衞：	有呀，我中文名叫白大衞。	**Daaihwaih:**	Yáuh a, ngóh Jūngmàhn méng giu Baahk Daaihwaih.
老師：	大衞，你係邊國人呀？	**Lóuhsī:**	Daaihwaih, néih haih bīngwok yàhn a?
大衞：	我係美國人，我係美國華僑。	**Daaihwaih:**	Ngóh haih Méihgwok yàhn, ngóh haih Méihgwok wàhkìuh.
老師：	你有十六個同學，一陣間介紹你識。	**Lóuhsī:**	Néih yáuh sahpluhk go tùhnghohk, yātjahngāan gaaisiuh néih sīk.
大衞：	好呀！	**Daaihwaih:**	Hóu a!

3. Vocabulary in use
活用詞彙 wuhtyuhng chìhwuih

3.1 Common vocabulary

Number	Word	Yale Romanization	POS	English
3.1.1	你好	néihhóu	PH	How are you?
3.1.2	叫	giu	V	to be called
3.1.3	乜嘢	mātyéh	QW	what
3.1.4	名	méng	N	name
3.1.5	我	ngóh	Pronoun	I, me, my
3.1.6	佢	kéuih	Pronoun	he, she, him, her
3.1.7	係	haih	V	to be

3.1.8	姓	sing	V	to have surname called
3.1.9	老師	lóuhsī	N	teacher
3.1.10	唔係	m̀haih	PH	not to be
3.1.11	美國人	Méihgwok yàhn	N	American
3.1.12	呀？	a？	Part	questioning particle
3.1.13	華僑	wàhkìuh	N	Overseas Chinese
3.1.14	呢？	nē？	Part	how about?
3.1.15	香港人	Hēungggóng yàhn	N	Hong Kong people
3.1.16	中文大學	Jūngmàhn Daaihhohk	N	The Chinese University of Hong Kong
3.1.17	學生	hohksāang	N	student
3.1.18	嘎？	àh？	Part	reconfirming particle
3.1.19	好	hóu	Adv	very
3.1.20	大	daaih	Adj	big
3.1.21	靚	leng	Adj	pretty
3.1.22	學	hohk	V	to learn
3.1.23	中文	Jūngmàhn	N	Chinese language
3.1.24	廣東話	Gwóngdūngwá	N	Cantonese language
3.1.25	英文	Yīngmàhn	N	English language
3.1.26	鍾意	jūngyi	V	to like
3.1.27	早晨	jóusàhn	PH	Good morning
3.1.28	班	bāan	N	class
3.1.29	有	yáuh	V	to have
3.1.30	冇	móuh	V	not to have
3.1.31	中文名	Jūngmàhn méng	N	Chinese name
3.1.32	邊國	bīngwok	QW	Which country?
3.1.33	一陣（間）	yātjahn (gāan)	PH	a while
3.1.34	介紹⋯識	gaaisiuh…sīk	V	to introduce

3.2 Proper nouns

3.2.1	大衛	Daaihwaih	Name	David
3.2.2	李	Léih	Surname	Lee
3.2.3	林	Làhm	Surname	Lam
3.2.4	子安	Jíōn	Name	Ji On
3.2.5	美國	Méihgwok	PW	America
3.2.6	香港	Hēunggóng	PW	Hong Kong
3.2.7	英國	Yīnggwok	PW	Britain
3.2.8	中國	Jūnggwok	PW	China
3.2.9	日本	Yahtbún	PW	Japan
3.2.10	韓國	Hòhngwok	PW	Korea

4. Notes on language structures
語言結構知識 yúhyìhn gitkau jīsīk

4.1 Pronunciation guide

Cantonese pronunciation & romanization: Initial, final and tones
Cantonese is a tonal language, in which tones play a very important role in identifying the meaning of words. There are many Romanization systems (around 10 common ones) used in Cantonese course books. This book uses the "Yale Romanization System".

A syllable in Cantonese is composed of 3 components:

1. An initial "sīngmóuh"– consonants used at the beginning of a syllable.
2. A final "wáhnmóuh"– the part of a syllable that follows an initial, it can be a vowel, vowel

glide or a combination of vowel and consonants

3. A tone "sīngdiuh" – the pitch contour of a syllable. There are 6 tones used in this book, i.e. ā, á, a, àh, áh, ah.

Cantonese Tones:

This book employs a six-tone system, which is accepted by many scholars. The six tones are high level; high rising; mid-level; low falling; low rising and low level. The tones are represented by diacritic marks written on top of the main vowels. Mid-level tone has no tone mark."h" is placed after the vowels to indicate low pitch tones and the "h" indicating low pitch tones are not pronounced. To make the tones visible, table 1. can show the pitch contour of the voice.

Table 1. Cantonese tones

Tone	High Level	High Rising	Mid-level	Low Falling	Low Rising	Low Level
Pitch	5 → 5	3 → 5	3 → 3	2 → 1	1 → 3	2 → 2
Tone Mark						

NOTE: Some people would use a high falling tone (53) for a high level one to stress certain words. However, the two tones do not make difference in the meaning of the word.

Table 2. Cantonese tones with examples

Tone	H.L.	H.R.	M.L.	L.F.	L.R.	L.L.
Romanization	sī	sí	si	sìh	síh	sih
English meaning	poem	history	try	time	market	be
Chinese Character	詩	史	試	時	市	是

SPELLING CONVENTION:

1. The tone mark of the "rising", "falling" or "high level" tone is placed on the top of the first vowel.

2. The not-pronounced "h" is placed behind the vowels of a final to indicate low pitch tones.
3. The mid-level and low level tones have no tone mark.

香
↓ High Level tone mark
h ēung
initial ▲ ▲ final

港
↓ High Rising tone mark
g óng
initial ▲ ▲ final

中
↓ High Level tone mark
j ūng
initial ▲ ▲ final

大
↓ (without tone mark for level tones)
↓ Low Pitch tone mark
d aaih
initial ▲ ▲ final

早
↓ High Rising tone mark
j óu
initial ▲ ▲ final

晨
↓ Falling tone mark
↓ Low Pitch tone mark
s àhn
initial ▲ ▲ final

Examples:

香 港	中 大	早 晨
Hēung góng	Jūng daaih	Jóu sàhn

4.2 Structure notes

4.2.1 Descriptive sentences: Subject-Verb-Object sentences

A basic descriptive sentence contains two parts, a subject and a predicate. See examples below.

Subject-(Adv.)-Adj. sentences

Subject	Predicate (Adj, Adv + Adj)	Subject	Predicate (Adj, Adv + Adj)
你	好	Néih	hóu
香港	靚	Hēunggóng	leng
美國	大	Méihgwok	daaih
王小姐	好靚	Wòhng síujé	hóu leng

Subject-Verb-Object sentences

Subject	Predicate (V, V + O)	Subject	Predicate (V, V + O)
我	叫大衛	Ngóh	giu Daaihwaih
你	係中文大學學生	Néih	haih Jūngmàhn Daaihhohk hohksāang
佢	姓王	Kéuih	sing Wòhng
大衛	學英文	Daaihwaih	hohk Yīngmàhn

4.2.2 Negative sentences

Negative sentence is formed by putting " 唔 m̀ " in front of the predicate or the verb. See examples below.

唔	m̀	唔係	m̀haih
唔好	m̀hóu	唔知道	m̀Jīdou
唔靚	m̀leng	唔學	m̀hohk

4.2.3   Questions forms
There are three types of yes-no questions in Cantonese, they are (1) ma-type questions, (2) choice-type questions and (3) àh-type questions.

4.2.3.1   ma-type questions

Cantonese yes-no questions can be ended with …ma?
Examples
Hēunggóng leng ma?
Néih jūngyi Hēunggóng ma?
Léih síujé leng ma?

4.2.3.2   Choice-type questions

In Cantonese, choice-type questions are very common in asking yes-no questions. Choice-type questions always end with particle "…a?"
Examples
Hēunggóng lengṁleng a?
Néih jūngṁjūngyi Hēunggóng a?
Léih síujé lengṁleng a?

4.2.3.3   àh-type questions

The particle "…àh?" is added to a statement to turn it into a question expecting confirmation, agreement or showing surprise. The answer to such questions should start with "haih" (meaning "yes") if the previous statement is correct, whereas it should start with "ṁhaih" (meaning "no") if the statement is incorrect.
Examples
Hēunggóng leng àh?
Néihṁjūngyi Hēunggóng àh?
Léih síujé hóu leng àh?

4.2.4   Sentences with 有 yáuh
The negative form of the verb "yáuh" is "móuh", and the choice-type question form should be "S yáuh móuh O a?".
Examples
Néih yáuh móuh syū a?

Kéuih yáuh móuh gòhgō a?

Néihdeih yáuh móuh XXX a?

4.2.5 Number – Measure – Noun structure (Nu-M-N)

In Chinese, every noun has its own measure word. When we talk about the quantity of a noun, the number must be followed by a measure word to serve as a modifier to the noun.

Examples

Yātgo yàhn

Léuhnggo hohksāang

Sāambūi gafē

Seibūi chàh

Luhkbún Jūngmàhn syū

4.2.6 Cantonese numbers (1-10)

0	1	2	3	4	5	6	7	8	9	10
lìhng	yāt	yih	sāam	sei	ńgh	luhk	chāt	baat	gáu	sahp

5. Notes on pragmatic knowledge

語用知識注解 yúhyuhng jīsīk jyugáai

5.1 How to greet people with similar status

5.1.1 Greeting expressions

Common greeting expressions is 你好 ! Néih hóu!.

Sometimes, Hong Kong people greet friends in casual situations using "Hi!" or " 哈佬 ! Hālóu!" (from Hello!)

5.1.2 Chinese names

In Chinese/Cantonese, family name should precede one's given name, and titles like "sīnsāang" (Mr.), "taaitáai" (Mrs), "síujé" (Miss) should go after one's surname or full name. In Hong Kong Cantonese, it will be safer to address a young lady "síujé" when you are not sure about her marital status.

In Mainland China, job titles like "haauhjéung" (school principal) or "gīngléih" (manager) can also be used to address people, such as "Wòhng gīngléīh".

The word " 姓 sing" (surname) is not just a noun in Cantonese, but use as a verb. Most of the time it appears as a verb in a sentence. In a formal situation, such as first meeting with one' superior, colleagues or guests, surname will be used with a title. See example below:

我姓何，係你地嘅老師。	Ngóh sing Hòh, haih néihdeihge lóuhsī.
你地嘅廣東話老師姓乜嘢呀？	Néihdeihge Gwōngdūngwá lóuhsī sing mātyéh a?
我地嘅廣東話老師姓李。	Ngóhdeihge Gwóngdūngwá lóuhsī sing Léih.
我唔係姓張，我姓李。	Ngóh m̀haih sing Jēung, ngóh sing Léih.

In very formal situations, " 你貴姓呀？ néih gwai sing a?" will be used to ask someone's surname to show respect to the person.

5.2 Related Knowledge

5.2.1 Omission of pronoun

In actual speech, personal pronouns in the second clause can be repeated for emphasis but it is possible to drop when the meaning can be inferred from the context. See examples below.

我姓馬，（我）叫馬雲。	Ngóh sing Máh, (ngóh) giu Máh Wàhn.
我叫馬雲，（我）係你地老師。	Ngóh giu Máh Wàhn, (Ngóh) haih néihdeih lóuhsī.
佢係我姐姐，（佢）叫馬麗。	Kéuih haih ngóh jèhjē, (kéuih) giu Máh Laih.

5.2.2 Starting questions with " 請問 chíngmahn/chéngmahn"

"請問 chíngmahn/chéngmahn…" means "may I ask…", which is a polite way to open a question or to make requests in Cantonese.

Examples:
Chéngmahn néih haihm̀haih Wòhng síujé a?
Chéngmahn néih haihm̀haih Máhwàhn a?

5.2.3 Saying "thank you" in Cantonese: "唔該 m̀gōi" verses"多謝 dōjeh"

Both "唔該 m̀gōi" and "多謝 dōjeh" can be translated into "thank you" in English. However the two phrases have different use according to different situations.

" 唔該 m̀gōi" is used to thank someone when someone has done you a favor or provided services for you.

" 多謝 dōjeh" is used to thank for gifts or thank for verbal compliments.

5.2.4 Good morning:Greeting people in the morning

" 早晨 jóusàhn" means "good morning". It is used to greet people in the morning. " 你好 néih hóu" means "how are you" and is used to greet people for any other time of the day.

6. Contextualized speaking practice

情境説話練習 chìhnggíng syutwah lihnjaahp

6.1 Pronunciation Exercises Faatyām lihnjààhp

6.1.1 The following is the Chinese names of continents in the world. Listen and read it aloud. Pay attention to the pronunciation of the tones in various combinations.

（1） 非洲	Fēijāu (Africa)	（1） 歐洲	Āu jāu (Europe)
（2） 南美洲	Nàahmméih jāu (South America)	（2） 北美洲	Bāk Méihjāu (North America)
（3） 亞洲	Ajāu (Asia)	（3） 大洋洲	Daaihyèuhng jāu (Oceania)
（4） 澳洲	Ou jāu (Australia)	（4） 南極洲	Nàahmgihk jāu(Antarctica)

6.1.2 The following is the Chinese names of countries in the world. Listen and read it aloud. Pay attention to the pronunciation of the 3rd tone in various combinations.

冰島	Bīngdóu (Iceland)	伊朗	Yīlóhng (Iran)
秘魯	Beilóuh (Peru)	瑞典	Seuihdín (Sweden)

也門	Yáhmùhn (Yemen)	緬甸	Míhndihn (Myanmar)
比利時	Béileihsìh (Belgium)	柬埔寨	Gáanpòuhjaaih (Cambodia)
巴拿馬	Bānàhmáh (Panama)	牙買加	Ngàhmáaihgā (Jamaica)
尼泊爾	Nèihpokyíh (Nepal)	土耳其	Tóuyíhkèih (Turkey)
斯里蘭卡	Sīléihlàahnkā (Sri Lanka)	保加利亞	BóugāleihA (Bulgaria)
馬來西亞	Máhlòihsāi'A (Malaysia)	委內瑞拉	Wáinoihseuihlāai (Venezuela)

6.2 Situational Topics Chìhnggíng syutwah lihnjaahp

Complete the following dialogues in the context of the situation described below.

6.2.1 Today is the first day of class and you want to know your classmates.
First collect information from your classmates by asking the questions below, and then complete the dialogue according to the information you collected.
今日係第一日上堂，你想認識你嘅同學。你問同學下面嘅問題，然後根據呢啲資料完成下面嘅對話。
Gamyaht haih daihyāt yaht séuhngtòhng, néih séung yihngsīk néihge tùhnghohk.Néih mahn tùhnghohk hahmihnge mahntàih, yìhnhauh gāngeui nīdī jīlíu yùhnsìhng hahmihnge deuiwah.

The information of your classmates

Question \ Name	Sing mātyéh a? 姓乜嘢呀？	Giu mātyéh méng a? 叫乜嘢呀？	Haihṁhaih… a? 係唔係⋯呀？	Hohk mātyéh a? 學乜嘢呀？

Please fill in the blanks in the following dialogue.

你：你好， 我叫＿＿＿＿＿。 你叫＿＿＿＿＿？	Néih: Néih hóu, Ngóh giu ＿＿＿＿＿. Néih giu ＿＿＿＿＿?
同學：你好， 我叫＿＿＿＿＿。	Tùhnghohk: Néih hóu, Ngóh giu ＿＿＿＿＿.
你：你係唔係＿＿＿＿＿呀？	Néih: Néih haihm̀haih ＿＿＿＿＿ a?
同學：唔係，我係＿＿＿＿＿。	Tùhnghohk: M̀haih, ngóh haih ＿＿＿＿＿.
你：你係唔係＿＿＿＿＿呀？	Néih: Néih haihm̀haih ＿＿＿＿＿ a?
同學：係，我係＿＿＿＿＿。	Tùhnghohk: haih, ngóh haih ＿＿＿＿＿.
你：我學＿＿＿＿＿。 你＿＿＿＿＿？	Néih: Ngóh hohk ＿＿＿＿＿. Néih ＿＿＿＿＿?
同學：我＿＿＿＿＿。	Tùhnghohk: Ngóh ＿＿＿＿＿.

6.2.2 You are chatting with your Chinese friend and your friend wants to know who your Chinese teacher is.

你嘅中國朋友想知道你嘅中文老師係邊個。

Néihge Jūnggwok pàhngyáuh séung jīdou néihge Jūngmàhn lóuhsī haih bīngo.

朋友：房老師＿＿＿＿你地嘅老師嘎？	Pàhngyáuh: Fòhng lóuhsī ＿＿＿＿ néihdeih ge lóuhsī àh?
你：唔係，我地嘅老師姓＿＿＿＿。	Néih: M̀haih, ngóhdeihge lóuhsī sing ＿＿＿＿.
朋友：李老師係＿＿＿＿嗎？	Pàhngyáuh: Léih lóuhsī haih ＿＿＿＿ ma?
你：係，＿＿＿＿係中國人。	Néih: Haih, ＿＿＿＿ haih Jūnggwok yàhn.

6.3 Speech topics

Please practice the following topics.

Néih gaaisiuhháh jihgéi béi néih gó bāan ge tùhnghohk, dōu gáandāan gónghàh néihge gwokgā.

你介紹吓自己俾你嗰班嘅同學識，都簡單講吓你嘅國家。

Please introduce yourself to your classmates and tell us something about your country.

Néih yáuh léuhnggo pàhngyáuh, daahnhaih kéuihdeih haihm̀sīk ge. Yìhgā chéng néih gaaisiuh kéuihdeih sīk lā.

你有兩個朋友，但係佢哋係唔識嘅，而家請你介紹佢哋識啦。

You have two friends, but they don't know each other. Now please introduce them to each other.

7 Listening and speaking

聽説練習 tingsyut lihnjaahp

7.1 At the school counter

大衛：	早晨！	**Daaihwaih:**	Jóusàhn!
職員：	早晨！請問你搵邊個呀？	**Jīkyùhn:**	Jóusàhn! Chíngmahn néih wán bīngo a?
大衛：	我搵李老師。	**Daaihwaih:**	Ngóh wán Léih lóuhsī.
職員：	請問你叫乜嘢名呀？	**Jīkyùhn:**	Chíngmahn néih giu mātyéh méng a?
大衛：	我叫白大衛，我係佢學生。我學廣東話。	**Daaihwaih:**	Ngóh giu Baahk Daaihwaih, ngóh haih kéuih hohksāang. Ngóh hohk Gwóngdūngwá.
職員：	好，請你等一陣。	**Jīkyùhn:**	Hóu, chíng néih dáng yātjahn.
大衛：	好，唔該你。	**Daaihwaih:**	Hóu, m̀gōi néih.

Lesson 2　Asking the way
問路指路

1. Contexts and linguistic functions
語境特徵與語言功能 yúhgíng dahkjīng yúh yúhyìhn gūngnàhng

Contexts (who, where, when) 語境特徵（人地時）	Linguistic functions 語言功能
Who: new acquaintance, new friend **Where:** school, casual gathering, office, etc **When:** first few encounters	**Core function:** Querying 詢問
Language Scenarios: General situations, e.g. find a place 一般情況，如尋找地方	**Supplementary function:** Explaining reasons 說明原因

Notes on pragmatic knowledge	Notes on language structures
I.　How to talk to a stranger 　　Greeting with: "heui bīndouh a?" 　　Saying goodbye in Cantonese II. Related knowledge 　　Asking for agreement using "hóu m̀hóu a?"	- Telling locations 　**S hái PW** 　**S hái PW VO** 　**S hái PW/N chìhnbihn…** 　**PW yáuh N** - Adverb jauh - jīdou vs sīk - Time word 　**(TW) S (TW) V O** 　**S géisìh V O a?** - Telling sequence of events with sīn… jīhauh - Cantonese numbers 1-99

2. Texts
課文 fomàhn

2.1 On school campus

子安：	大衛、安娜，你地去邊度呀？	**Jíōn:**	Daaihwaih, Ōnnàh, néihdeih heui bīndouh a?
安娜：	我去上堂。	**Ōnnàh:**	Ngóh heui séuhngtòhng.
大衛：	我去做運動，你呢？	**Daaihwaih:**	Ngóh heui jouh wahnduhng, néih nē?
子安：	我去餐廳食飯。聽日見。	**Jíōn:**	Ngóh heui chāantēng sihkfaahn. Tīngyaht gin.
大衛：	聽日見。	**Daaihwaih:**	Tīngyaht gin.
安娜：	再見。	**Ōnnàh:**	Joigin.

2.2 Near the train station

子安：	請問，大學站係唔係喺前邊呀？	**Jíōn:**	Chíngmahn, Daaihhohk jaahm haihm̀haih hái chìhnbihn a?
路人A：	係呀，（大學車站）就喺前邊。	**Louhyàhn A:**	Haih a, (Daaihhohk chējaahm) jauh hái chìhnbihn.
子安：	唔該。你知唔知道超級市場喺邊度呀？	**Jíōn:**	M̀gōi. Néih jīm̀jī chīukāp síhchèuhng hái bīndouh a?
路人A：	知道，喺山上邊，喺餐廳旁邊。	**Louhyàhn A:**	Jīdou, hái sāan seuhngbihn, hái chāantēng pòhngbīn.
子安：	呢度有冇廁所呀？	**Jíōn:**	Nīdouh yáuh móuh chisó a?
路人A：	對唔住，我唔知(道)。	**Louhyàhn A:**	Deuim̀jyuh, ngóhm̀jī (dou).
子安：	唔緊要。	**Jíōn:**	M̀gányiu.

大衛：	你知唔知道博物館喺邊度呀？	**Daaihwaih:**	Néih jīm̀jīdou bokmaht gún hái bīndouh a?
路人B：	知道，喺辦公大樓左邊。	**Louhyàhn B:**	Jīdou, hái baahngūng daaihlàuh jóbihn.
路人C：	唔係，喺圖書館後邊。	**Louhyàhn C:**	M̀haih, hái tòuhsyū gún hauhbihn.
路人D：	都唔係，博物館喺火車站後邊。	**Louhyàhn D:**	Dōu m̀haih, bokmaht gún hái fóchē jaahm hauhbihn.

2.3 In the dormitory

大衛：	小文，想唔想去睇戲呀？聽講呢齣電影好好睇。	**Daaihwaih:**	Síumàhn, séungm̀séung heui táihei a? tēnggóng nīchēut dihnyíng hóu hóu tái.
小文：	好呀，你想幾時去呀？	**Síumàhn:**	Hóu a, néih séung géisìh heui a?
大衛：	今晚，好唔好？	**Daaihwaih:**	Gāmmáahn, hóum̀hóu?
小文：	今晚唔得。聽日有考試，我要溫習。	**Síumàhn:**	Gāmmáahnm̀dāk. Tīngyaht yáuh háausíh, ngóh yiu wānjaahp.
大衛：	噉，聽晚呢？	**Daaihwaih:**	Gám, tīngmáahn nē?
小文：	聽晚冇問題。	**Síumàhn:**	Tīngmáahn móuh mahntàih.
大衛：	好，就聽晚去。	**Daaihwaih:**	Hóu, jauh tīngmáahn heui.
小文：	好，聽日見。	**Síumàhn:**	Hóu, tīngyaht gin.

3. Vocabulary in use

活用詞彙 wuhtyuhng chìhwuih

3.1 Common vocabulary

Number	Word	Yale Romanization	POS	English
3.1.1	你地	néihdeih	N	you (plural)
3.1.2	去	heui	V	to go
3.1.3	邊度	bīndouh	QW	where?
3.1.4	上堂	séuhngtòhng	V	to go to class
3.1.5	做運動	jouh wahnduhng	V	to do sports
3.1.6	餐廳	chāantēng	N	restaurant
3.1.7	食飯	sihkfaahn	V	to have meal
3.1.8	聽日見	tīngyaht gin	PH	see you tomorrow
3.1.9	再見	joigin	PH	see you again
3.1.10	請問	chíngmahn	PH	would like to ask…
3.1.11	喺	hái	V	to be located
3.1.12	前邊	chìhnbihn	N	in front
3.1.13	唔該	m̀gōi	PH	thank you
3.1.14	知道	jīdou	V	to know
3.1.15	上邊	seuhngbihn	N	on top
3.1.16	旁邊	pòhngbīn	N	next to, beside
3.1.17	呢度	nīdouh	PW	here
3.1.18	對唔住	deui m̀jyuh	PH	sorry
3.1.19	唔緊要	m̀gányiu	PH	never mind, no problem
3.1.20	左邊	jóbihn	N	left
3.1.21	後邊	hauhbihn	N	behind
3.1.22	想	séung	AV	want to

3.1.23	睇戲	táihei	V	to watch movie
3.1.24	聽講	tēnggóng	PH	I heard that…
3.1.25	電影	dihnyíng	N	movie
3.1.26	幾時	géisìh	QW	when?
3.1.27	今晚	gāmmāan / gāmmáahn	TW	tonight
3.1.28	唔得	m̀dāk	PH	not ok
3.1.29	聽晚	tīngmáahn	TW	tomorrow night
3.1.30	考試	háausíh	N	examination
3.1.31	要	yiu	AV/V	have to, to need
3.1.32	溫習	wānjaahp	V	to review, to study
3.1.33	噉	gám	Part	then
3.1.34	冇問題	móuh mahntàih	PH	no problem

3.2 Proper nouns

3.2.1	安娜	Ōnnàh	Name	Anna
3.2.2	小文	Síumàhn	Name	Siu Man
3.2.3	大學站	Daaihhohk jaahm	PW/N	University station
3.2.4	超級市場	chīukāp síhchèuhng	PW/N	supermarket
3.2.5	廁所	chisó	PW/N	toilet
3.2.6	博物館	bokmahtgún	PW/N	museum
3.2.7	辦公大樓	baahngūng daaihlàuh	PW/N	office building
3.2.8	圖書館	tòuhsyūgún	PW/N	library
3.2.9	火車站	fóchē jaahm	PW/N	train station

4. Notes on language structures

語言結構知識 *yúhyìhn gitkau jīsīk*

4.1 Pronunciation guide

Cantonese initials:

There are 19 initials in present-day's Cantonese sound system. According to the phonetic features, the 19 initials can be divided into 5 groups. Learners should notice the following points in pronouncing or listening to the initials.

The "j" and "ch" are pronounced with lips spread, instead of rounded or protruded lips. The "ch" and "j" initials in Cantonese such as in "chàh" (tea) and "jyuh" (to live in a place) are not the same as those in "church" and "judge" in English.

Some sociolinguistic research shows that Cantonese speakers may pronounce initial "n" like "l", such as "néuihyán" (woman) as "léuihyán".

The "g" resembles the "c" in "scan" in English.

The "kw" is a strong aspirated sound, resembling "qu" in "quick" in English.

The "ng" initial resembles the sound of "ng" in "singer" in English". Sociolingustic observation shows young Cantonese speakers may drop the initial "ng", as in "ngóh" (I, me) and pronounced like "óh"

Initial "y" sounds similar to the "y" in "yes" in English.

Sociolinguistic research also shows some natives Cantonese speakers may pronounce initial "gw" without rounded lips, as "gwok" (country) may be pronounced as "gok".

Table 3. The 19 initials in Cantonese in 5 groups.

Group	Initials	Chinese characters	Romanization	English meaning
1	**Aspired stops**			
	p	怕	pa	afraid
	t	太	taai	too much
	k	咭	kāat	card

| ch | 差 | chā | bad |
| kw | 裙 | kwàhn | skirt |

2   Unaspirated stops

b	爸	bā	father
d	打	dá	hit
g	家	gā	home
j	炸	ja	bombard
gw	掛	gwa	hang

3   Nasals

m	馬	máh	horse
n	那	náh	that
ng	我	ngóh	I, me

4   Fricatives & Continuants

f	花	fā	flower
s	沙	sā	sand
h	蝦	hā	shrimp
l	喇	la	sentence particle

5   Semi-vowels

| y | 也 | yáh | also |
| w | 話 | wá | language |

4.2 Structure notes

4.2.1 Telling locations

"hái" in Cantonese means "in", "on", or "at". "hái" must come before the place word.

S hái PW

Examples

Kéuih hái hohkhaauh.

Kéuihge pàhngyáuh hái Méihgwok.

Néihge ūkkéi (home) hái bīndouh a?

"hái" serves as a co-verb to indicate where an action takes place.

S hái PW VO

Examples

Ngóh pàhngyáuh hái Hēunggóng hohk Gwóngdūngwá.

Ngóh hái ūkkéi fangaau.

Néihdeih hái bīndouh sihkfaahn a?

In Cantonese, when telling location, the word order must be:

S hái PW/N chìhnbihn...

Examples

Kéuihge hohkhaauh hái fóchē jaahm chìhnbihn.

Néihge ūkkéi hái bindouh a?

Ngóhge ūkkéi hái fóchē jaahm seuhngbihn

In Cantonese, existential sentences can be formed by using "yáuh" meaning "there is/ are...". Place word is put before "yáuh", as in "PW yáuh...", to show that "there is/are... in the place".

PW yáuh N

PW móuh N is the negative form showing that there is/are no N in the place.

Examples

Hohkhaauh yáuh hóudō Méihgwok hohksāang.

Ngóh ūkkéi fuhgahn (nearby) móuh fóchē jaahm.

Fóchē jaahm léuihbihn móuh chisó.

The choice-type question form is "PW yáuh móuh N a?"

Examples

Sātìhn yáuh móuh chàhlàuh (Chinese teahouse) a?

Fóchē jaahm yáuh móuh chisó a?

Néih ūkkéi yáuh móuh yàhn a?

4.2.2 Adverb 就 Jauh

Adverb "jauh" is used to indicate immediacy.

Examples

Chìhnbihn jauh haih fóchē jaahm.

Ngóh ūkkéi jauh hái chìhnbihn.

Tīngyaht jauh háausíh.

4.2.3 To know: 知道 Jīdou vs 識 sīk

Both "jīdou 知道 " and "sīk 識 " can be translated into "to know" in English. However the meanings and use of "jīdou 知道 " and "sīk 識 " are different. "sīk 識 " is used to indicate that you know someone, e.g. "ngóh sīk Edmond" (I know Edmond); or to show that you know some skills, e.g. "ngóh sīk yàuhséui" (I know how to swim).

"Jīdou 知道 " is usually followed by a statement, e.g. "ngóh jīdou kéuih haih Wòhng lóuhsī" (I know he/she is Teacher Wong); or followed by a factual statement, e.g. "ngóh m̀jīdou kéuih haih bīngo" (I don't know who he/she is).

4.2.4 Time words

Time words in Cantonese can be put before or after the sentence subject.

(TW) S (TW) V O

Examples

Ngóhdeih tīngyaht háausíh.

Gāmyaht néih hái bīndouh sihkfaahn a?

Ngóh gāmyaht hái ūkkéi sihkfaahn.

"géisìh" is a question word asking "when". It should also be placed before or after the sentence subject.

S géisìh V O a?

Examples

Néihdeih géisìh háausíh a?

Ngóhdeih géisìh heui sihkfaahn a?

Néihge pàhngyáuh géisìh hái Hēunggóng a?

4.2.5 Measure words/classifier 個 go

In Cantonese, all nouns have at least one measure word, which is also known as classifiers, when the nouns are being specified or counted. Some nouns have more than one classifiers, depending on the nature of the object or of the things they are denoting. In informal speech, the classifier 個 go is used as a general or default classifier for most of the nouns.

Nu M (N)

Example

Yāt go pìhnggwó

Léuhng go yàhn

Sāam go pàhngyáuh

4.2.6 Telling sequence of events with ⋯之後 jīhauh⋯

The use of " 之後 jīhauh" can form longer sentences showing the temporal sequences of two actions.

Examples.

Ngóhdeih sihkfaahn jīhauh heui Sātìhn.

Háausíh jīhauh heui táihei, hóuṁhóu a?

Ngóhdeih heui Sātìhn táihei, jīhauh heui bīndouh a?

4.2.7 Cantonese numbers 1-99

11-19

11	12	13	14	...	18	19
sahpyāt	sahpyih	sahpsāam	sahpsei		sahpbaat	sahpgáu

2-9 + sahp

20	30	40	...	80	90
yihsahp	sāamsahp	seisahp		baatsahp	gáusahp

21-99

Examples

21	32	46	99
yihsahp yāt	sāamsahp yih	seisahp luhk	gáusahp gáu

The contracted form of "sahp"- "…ah…" in double digit numbers

21	Yihsahp yāt	→	Yahyāt
32	Sāamsahp yih	→	Sā'ah yih
46	Seisahp luhk	→	Sei'ah luhk
99	Gáusahp gáu	→	Gáu'ah gáu

5. Notes on pragmatic knowledge
語用知識注解 *yúhyuhng jīsīk jyugáai*

5.1 How to talk to a stranger

5.1.1. Greeting with: heui bīndouh a? 去邊度呀？

"heui bīndouh a? 去邊度呀？" is used as greeting among friends, colleagues and neighbors you know well. It does not matter what answer you give in response. The person asking is not intended to intrude your privacy. It will sound awkward if you greet someone superior to you, such as your teacher and your boss using this expression.

5.1.2 Saying goodbye in Cantonese

"joigin" is always the right word to use while saying goodbye to someone. However, you can also use "yātjahn gin" (see you in a while) or "chìhdī gin" (see you later) to someone you will meet again very soon.

5.2 Related knowledge

5.2.1 Asking for agreement using 好唔好呀？hóu m̀hóu a?

In Cantonese, you can add " 好 唔 好 呀 ？hóu m̀hóu a?" at the end of your suggestions or offer (a declarative sentence) to ask for agreement. It functions like a question tag as in English. In response, you can use "hóu" or "hóu a" in less formal speech to show a positive answer to show your agreement. Or you can use "m̀hóu", meaning "no good" or "not good", in less formal speech to show a negative answer to show disagreement. Normally an explanation will be given after the disagreement as a polite response to the suggestions or offer.

5.2.2. The treatment of two-syllable verbs in V-not-V questions

The original form of choice-type questions (V-not-V questions) with two-syllable verbs or two-syllable auxiliary verbs is XX-not-XX, which can be found in historical documents. The form has then been developed into X-not-XX in modern Cantonese, e.g. in "néih jīm̀jīdou kéuih haih bīngo a?" (Do you know who he/she is?")

6. Contextualized speaking practice

情境說話練習 chìhnggíng syutwah lihnjaahp

6.1 Pronunciation Exercises and Situational Topics

6.1.1 Your friend wants to know on which floor the Chinese teachers' office, the American restaurant and Chinese classroom are in this building. Answer your friend's questions according to the information provided below. Pay attention to the tones.

大廈指南 Daaihhàh jínàhm (Building Directory)		
10/F	Sahp láu 十樓	Gwóngdūngwá fosāt 廣東話課室
9/F	Gáu láu 九樓	Yīngmàhn fosāt, chisó 英文課室、廁所
8/F	Baat láu 八樓	Gwóngdūng wá lóuhsī ge baahngūngsāt 廣東話老師嘅辦公室

7/F	Chāt láu 七樓	Yīngmàhn lóuhsī ge baahngūngsāt, chisó 英文老師嘅辦公室、廁所
6/F	Luhk láu 六樓	Tòuhsyū gún (library) 圖書館
5/F	Ńgh láu 五樓	Gafēsāt (café), chisó 咖啡室、廁所
4/F	Sei láu 四樓	syūdim (bookstore) 書店
3/F	Sāam láu 三樓	Méihgwok chāantēng, chisó 美國餐廳、廁所
2/F	Yih láu 二樓	chàhlàuh 茶樓
1/F	Yāt láu 一樓	Chīukāp síhchèuhng (supermarket), chisó 超級市場、廁所

6.1.2 Answer the following questions according to the information provided above. Pay attention to the tones.

(1) 請問，超級市場係唔係喺七樓呀？	Chíngmahn, chīukāp síhchèuhng haihm̀haih hái chāt láu a?
Ans:_____。	Ans:_____。
(2) 請問，咖啡室係唔係喺九樓呀？	Chíngmahn, gafē sāt haihm̀haih hái gáu láu a?
Ans:_____。	Ans:_____。
(3) 請問，圖書館係唔係喺四樓？	Chíngmahn, tòuhsyū gún haihm̀haih hái sei láu?
Ans:_____。	Ans:_____。

6.1.3 You are looking for the classroom of Chinese lesson. Complete the following dialogue according to the situation.

你搵中文課嘅課室。根據呢個情況完成以下對話。

你：你好。請問，嗰個 _____ 中文課嘅課室？	Néih: néih hóu, chíngmahn gó go _____ jūngmàhn fo ge fosāt?
同學：唔係，中文課嘅課室喺 _____ 。	Tùhnghohk: M̀haih, Jūngmàhn fo ge fosāt hái _____ .
你：_____ 。	Néih: _____ .
同學：唔駛客氣。	Tùhnghohk: M̀sái haakhei.

6.1.4 It is early morning and you need to talk to your Chinese teacher, Mr. Wong before class. Now you are talking to the staff at the front desk.

朝早，你喺辦公室櫃台前邊，你同職員講你要搵黃老師。

你：_____ 。我搵黃老師。_____ ，黃老師 _____ 辦公室？	Néih: _____ . Ngóh wán Wòhng lóuhsī. _____ , Wòhng lóuhsī _____ baahngūngsāt?
職員：_____ ，佢喺辦公室。請問，你 _____ ？	Jīkyùhn: _____ , kéuih hái baahngūngsāt. Chíngmahn, néih _____ ?
你：我叫 _____ ，係佢嘅 _____ 。	Néih: Ngóh giu _____ , haih kéuihge _____ .
職員：好，請 _____ 。	Jīkyùhn: Hóu, chíng _____ .
你：唔該。	Néih: M̀gōi.

6.1.5 At a friend's party, you met a Chinese friend, Wòhng Jíōn. You two are exchanging names and sharing some personal information.

喺朋友嘅聚會上，你認識咗一個中國人，王子安。你地……

你：你好。我係 _____ 。你叫 _____ ？	Néih: Néih hóu. Ngóh haih _____ . Néih giu _____ ?
子安：我叫王子安。你係邊度人呀？	Jíōn: Ngóh giu Wòhng Jíōn. Néīh haih bīndouh yàhn a?
你：我係 _____ 人。你 _____ ？	Néih: Ngóh haih _____ yàhn. Néih _____ ?

子安：我係香港人。　　　　　　　　Jíōn: Ngóh haih Hēunggóng yàhn.

你：你係學生 _____ ?　　　Néih: Néih haih hohksāang _____ ?

子安：係，　　　　　　　　　　　　Jíōn: Haih,
我係 _____ 嘅學生。　　　　　　　Ngóh haih _____ ge hohksāang.

你：你 _____ ?　　　　　　Néih: Néih _____ ?

子安：我學英文。　　　　　　　　　Jíōn: Ngóh hohk Yīngmàhn.

你：你 _____ 英文名？　　　　　　Néih: Néih _____ Yīngmàhn méng?

子安：有，我叫 _____ 。　　　Jíōn: Yáuh, ngóh-giu _____ .

6.1.6　You just relocated to a new place. The following are the things you need to do today.
1) Open a bank account 2) Buy food in a supermarket 3) Go to your Chinese class
You are at the front gate of your dormitory now. Please complete the dialogue.

你：請問，呢度 _____ 銀行呀？　　Néih: Chíngmahn, nīdouh _____
　　　　　　　　　　　　　　　　　ngàhnhòhng a?

路人：有，就 _____ 。　　　　　Louhyàhn: Yáuh, jauh _____ .

你：唔該。你知唔知道超級市場　　　Néih: M̀gōi. Néih jīm̀jīdou chīukāp
喺 _____ 呀？　　　　　　　　　síhchèuhng hái _____ a?

路人：知道，超級市場 _____ 嘅後邊。　Louhyàhn: Jīdou, chīukāp síhchèuhng
　　　　　　　　　　　　　　　　　_____ ge hauhbihn.

你：請問，你知唔知道 _____ ?　Néih: Chíngmahn, néih jīm̀jīdou _____ ?

路人： _____ ，我都唔知道。　　　Louhyàhn: _____ , ngóh dōu
　　　　　　　　　　　　　　　　　m̀jīdou.

你：好， _____ 。　　　　　　　Néih: Hóu, _____ .

6.1.7 On your way home, you happen to meet your Chinese friend Síumàhn. Síumàhn and you exchange greetings.

返緊屋企，你見到一個中國朋友小文，你地打招呼。

小文：_____，你好， 你去邊度呀？	Síumàhn: _____, néih hóu, Néih heui bīndouh a ?
你：我 _____， 你 _____？	Néih: Ngóh _____, néih _____？
小文：我而家 _____。	Síumàhn: Ngóh yìhgā _____.
你：好，_____。	Néih: Hóu, _____.
小文：聽日見。	Síumàhn: Tīngyaht gin .

6.1.8 On your way to class, you happen to meet your Chinese teacher.
You are responding to teacher's greeting.

去緊課室，你見到你嘅中文老師，你同老師打招呼。

老師：_____，你好， 而家去上堂嗄？	Lóuhsī: _____, néih hóu, yìhgā heui séuhngtòhng àh?
學生：_____好。 _____。	Hohksāang: _____ hóu. _____.
老師：好，聽日見。	Lóuhsī:Hóu, tīngyaht gin.
學生：_____。	Hohksāang: _____.

6.2 Speech Topics

1. Chéng néih wah béi néihge Hēunggóng pàhngyáuh tēng néih hái hohkhaauh hohk Gwóngdūngwá ge chìhngyìhng (situation).

請你話俾你嘅香港朋友聽你喺學校學廣東話嘅情形。

Please tell your friend in Hong Kong about your Cantonese class in this school.

2. Néih gindóu daihyih bāan ge yātgo chōbāan hohksāang, néih wah béi kéuih tēng néih ge bāan ge chìhngyìhng. Néih dōu hóyíh mahnháh kéuih ge bāan ge chìhngyìhng.

你見倒第二班嘅一個初班學生，你話俾佢聽你嘅班嘅情形，你都可以問吓佢嘅班嘅情形。

You come across a beginning student from another class. You tell him/her about your class. You can also ask about his/her class.

7. Listening and speaking

聽説練習 tingsyut lihnjaahp

7.1 Near the dormitory

阿美：	小文，你去邊度呀？	A Mēi:	Síumàhn, néih heui bīndouh a?
小文：	我想返宿舍瞓覺。你呢？	Síumàhn:	Ngóh séung fāan sūkse fangaau. Néih nē?
阿美：	我去圖書館先，之後返宿舍。	A Mēi:	Ngóh heui tòuhsyū gún sīn, jīhauh fāan sūkse.
小文：	好，一陣見。	Síumàhn:	Hóu, yātjahn gin.
阿美：	一陣見。	A Mēi:	Yātjahn gin.

Lesson 3 Going out to have fun
出去玩下

1. Contexts and linguistic functions
語境特徵與語言功能 *yúhgíng dahkjīng yúh yúhyìhn gūngnàhng*

Contexts (who, where, when) 語境特徵 (人地時)	Linguistic functions 語言功能
Who: new friends, new acquaintance **Where:** restaurants, shops, etc **When:** first few encounters	**Core functions:** Inviting (informal) 邀約（非正式）
Language Scenarios: General situations, e.g. in restaurants, in Chinese restaurants, in shops 一般情況，如在餐廳、酒樓、商店	**Supplementary functions:** Expressing opinion 説自己意見

Notes on pragmatic knowledge	Notes on language structures

I. What to say when going out with friends
  1. Welcome greetings in shops
  2. The use of "yiu" vs "séung yiu"
II. Related knowledge
  1. The use of "yáuhdī"
	- Specified nouns
	- The use of "yātdī" and "yáuh (yāt) dī"
	- **N ge N**
	- "dihnghaih" structure
	- Auxiliary verb "séung", verb "yiu" and auxiliary verb "yiu"
	- Cantonese numbers 100 onwards
	- "daih" as a prefix
	- Questions formed with "nē?"

2. Texts

課文 fomàhn

2.1 In the dormitory

子安：	周末你想做乜嘢呀？	**Jíōn:**	Jāumuht néih séung jouh mātyéh a?
安娜：	我想去海邊玩下。你去唔去？	**Ōnnàh:**	Ngóh séung heui hóibīn wáanháh. Néih heuiṁheui?
子安：	呢個周末我要教英文。	**Jíōn:**	Nīgo jāumuht ngóh yiu gaau Yīngmàhn.
安娜：	噉，我地聽日去啦。聽日你有冇時間呀？	**Ōnnàh:**	Gám, ngóhdeih tīngyaht heui lā. Tīngyaht néih yáuh móuh sìhgaan a?
子安：	我聽日上晝考試，下晝有時間。	**Jíōn:**	Ngóh tīngyaht seuhngjau háausíh, hahjau yáuh sìhgaan.
安娜：	好呀，我地聽日下晝去啦。	**Ōnnàh:**	Hóu a, ngóhdeih tīngyaht hahjau heui lā.

2.2 On school campus

阿美：	今日係大衛生日。	**A Mēi:**	Gāmyaht haih Daaihwaih sāangyaht.
子安：	大衛，生日快樂，我請你食飯。	**Jíōn:**	Daaihwaih, sāangyaht faailohk, ngóh chéng néih sihkfaahn.
大衛：	好呀。多謝。	**Daaihwaih:**	Hóu a. Dōjeh.
子安：	你想食乜嘢呀？	**Jíōn:**	Néih séung sihk mātyéh a?
大衛：	我乜嘢都食。	**Daaihwaih:**	Ngóh mātyéh dōu sihk
子安：	噉，我地去飲茶啦。	**Jíōn:**	Gám, ngóhdeih heui yámchàh lā.

2.3 In the canteen

店員：	歡迎光臨，請問想食啲乜嘢呀？	**Dimyùhn:**	Fūnyìhng gwōnglàhm, chíngmahn séung sihk dī mātyéh a?
顧客：	我想要四份吞拿魚三文治。	**Guhaak:**	Ngóh séung yiu seifahn tānnàhyú sāammàhnjih.
店員：	對唔住，吞拿魚三文治賣晒啦。	**Dimyùhn:**	Deui m̀jyuh, tānnàhyú sāammàhnjih maaihsaai la.
顧客：	噉，要牛肉三文治啦。	**Guhaak:**	Gám, yiu ngàuhyuhk sāammàhnjih lā.
店員：	好，想飲乜嘢？要可樂、果汁定係咖啡？	**Dimyùhn:**	Hóu, séung yám mātyéh? Yiu hólohk, gwójāp dihnghaih gafē?
顧客：	要兩杯可樂同兩杯咖啡。	**Guhaak:**	Yiu léuhng būi hólohk tùhng léuhng būi gafē
店員：	咖啡，要凍嘅定係熱嘅？	**Dimyùhn:**	Gafē, yiu dungge dihnghaih yihtge?
顧客：	要熱嘅。	**Guhaak:**	Yiu yihtge.
店員：	好，請你等一陣。	**Dimyùhn:**	Hóu, chíng néih dáng yātjahn.

3 Vocabulary in use
活用詞彙 wuhtyuhng chìhwuih

3.1 Common vocabulary

Number	Word	Yale Romanization	POS	English
3.1.1	周末	jāumuht	TW	weekend
3.1.2	海邊	hóibīn	PW	sea side
3.1.3	玩下	wáanháh	PH	to have fun
3.1.4	呢個	nīgo	SP	this one

3.1.5	教	gaau	V	to teach
3.1.6	時間	sìhgaan	N	time
3.1.7	上晝	seuhngjau	TW	before noon
3.1.8	下晝	hahjau	TW	afternoon
3.1.9	啦	lā	P	sentence particle showing suggestions
3.1.10	今日	gāmyaht	TW	today
3.1.11	生日	sāangyaht	V	birthday
3.1.12	生日快樂	Sāangyaht faailohk	PH	Happy birthday
3.1.13	請你食飯	chéng néih sihkfaahn	PH	buy you meal
3.1.14	多謝	dōjeh	PH	thank you
3.1.15	乜嘢都食	mātyéh dōu sihk	PH	can eat anything
3.1.16	飲茶	yámchàh	V	to have dimsum (lit. to drink tea)
3.1.17	歡迎光臨	fūnyìhng gwōnglàhm	PH	welcome
3.1.18	吞拿魚三文治	tānnàh yú sāammàhnjih	N	tuna fish sandwiches
3.1.19	賣晒	maaihsaai	PH	Sold out
3.1.20	牛肉三文治	ngàuhyuhk sāammàhnjih	N	beef sandwiches
3.1.21	飲	yám	V	to drink
3.1.22	可樂	hólohk	N	Cola
3.1.23	果汁	gwójāp	N	fruit juice
3.1.24	咖啡	gafē	N	coffee
3.1.25	定係	dihnghaih	Patt	or
3.1.26	杯	būi	N/M	cup
3.1.27	凍	dung	Adj	cold
3.1.28	熱	yiht	Adj	hot
3.1.29	等	dáng	V	to wait

4 Notes on language structures

語言結構知識 *yúhyìhn gitkau jīsīk*

4.1 Pronunciation guide

Cantonese finals:

There are 51 finals in Cantonese (Yale Romanization). Within the 51 finals, there are short vowels, long vowels, diphthongs (vowel glides) and vowels with combinations with consonant-endings.

1. Cantonese has single vowels sounds, e.g. "a", "e", "i", "o", "u", "eu"&"yu"; and diphthongs, e.g. "ai", "ou", "aau"… When the single vowel has no following consonant-endings, they are supposed to the pronounced as long vowels, e.g. "ma", "me", "mi", "mo"&"mu".

2. There is a distinction between diphthongs having short vowel "a" (spelt as "a") and those having long vowel"a" (spelt as "aa").

3. The finals "eu", "eung", "euk", "eui", "eun" and "eut" are rounded central vowels. For example, "hēu" (boot); "sēut" (shirt); "seun" (letter); "heui" (to go); "lèuhng" (cool) and "yeuhk" (medicine).

4. The endings "-p", "-t" and "-k" are unreleased stops.

5. The "i" in Cantonese is different from the one in English, as the tongue position is higher, for example, "tīn" (sky) comparing with the English word "teen".

6. The "o" is similar to "o" as in "got" in English, pronounced with rounded lips, for example, "ló" (to get).

7. The "u" is also similar to the vowel as in "wood" in English, pronounced with rounded lips, for example, "luhk" (green).

4.2 Structure notes

4.2.1 Specified nouns

In Cantonese, all specifier "nī", "gó" and "bīn" must be followed by measures.

SP M (N)

Examples

nīgo pìhnggwó

gógo yàhn

gódī pàhngyáuh

A number (Nu) can be added between the specifier ("nī", "gó"&"bīn") and the measure, indicating the amount of the noun specified.

SP Nu M (N)
Examples
nī sāam go yàhn
gó léuhng go hohksāang
Bīn sei bún syū… a?

4.2.2   The use of "yātdī" and "yáuh (yāt) dī"
Both "yātdī" and "yáuhdī" mean "some". "yáuhdī" is placed in the subject position meaning "some of the …", e.g. "yáuhdī yàhn haih Méihgwok yàhn".

4.2.3   Noun phrases with " 嘅 ge"
"ge" is a possessive marker. When "ge" is placed after a noun to indicate possessiveness, e.g. "ngóh ge pàhngyáuh" (my friend).

N ge N
Examples
ngóh ge pàhngyáuh
kéuih ge bàhbā
néih ge syū

"ge" can be placed after the adjective to modify nouns.

Adj ge N
Adv Adj ge N
Examples
hóu leng ge hóibīn
hóusihkge sāammàhnjih
lengge sāam (clothes)

"ge" can be used with nouns, pronouns, adjectives and verbs or verb phrases to form a nominal phrase. The nouns after "ge" can be omitted if the nouns had been mentioned in previous contexts in the speech. However, "ge" cannot be omitted in cases when the noun being modified is omitted. And "ge" cannot be omitted when an adverb is used to modify the adjective.

Examples

nībūi hólohk haih néih ge, m̀haih ngóh ge.

Daaihhohk yáuh hóuhóu ge bokmahtgún, dōu yáuh hóudaaih ge tòuhsyūgún.

4.2.4 "定係 dihnghaih" structure

"定係 dihnghaih" is similar to "or" in English, indicating a choice. Using "定係 dihnghaih" can form a question which offer a choice between two (or more) alternatives, and the alternatives are joined by " 定係 dihnghaih".

Examples

Néih yiu gafē dihnghaih chàh a?

Néih tīngyaht dihnghaih hauhyaht dākhàahn a?

Ngóhdeih heui sātìhn dihnghaih Jīmsājéui sihkfaahn a?

4.2.5 Auxiliary verb "想 séung" , verb "要 yiu" and auxiliary verb "要 yiu"

" 想 séung" used as a auxiliary verb has a meaning of "want", e.g. "néih séung sihk mātyéh a?" (What do you want to eat?).

Séung V

Séung VO

Examples

Ngóh séung fangaau.

Ngóh m̀séung sihkfaahn.

Kéuih m̀dākhàahn, Kéuih m̀séung heui Sātìhn. Néih séungm̀séung heui a?

When " 要 yiu" is used as a verb, it means "want to have something".

Yiu N

Examples

Ngóh yiu dung gafē (iced coffee).

Kéuih yiu hólohk (Cola).

Néihdeih yiu mātyéh a?

When " 要 yiu" is used as an auxiliary verb, it means "need to do something".

Yiu V
Yiu VO
Examples

Ngóh gāmyaht yiu háausíh, m̀dākhàahn a!

Ngóh yiu heui Sātìhn máaihyéh, néih heui m̀heui a?

Néih gāmyaht yiu jouh mātyéh a?

4.2.6   Cantonese number 100 onwards

Over one hundred: Nu baak + (01-99)

Examples

162 yātbaak luhksahp yih

458 seibaak ńghsahp baat

Over one thousand: Nu chīn + (01-999)

Examples

1,346 yātchīn sāambaak seisahp luhk

8,631 baatchīn luhkbaak sāamsahp yāt

3,409 sāamchīn seibaak lìhng gáu

Over ten thousand: Nu maahn + (01-9999)

Examples

12,987 yātmaahn yihchīn gáubaak baatsahp chāt

43,231 seimaahn sāamchīn yihbaak sāamsahp yāt

910,983 gáusahp yātmaahn lìhng gáubaak baatsahp sāam

6,381,321 luhkbaat sāamsahp baatmaahn yātchīn sāambaak yihsahp yāt

76,407, 690 chātchīn luhkbaak seisahpmaahn chātchīn luhkbaak gáusahp

Over one hundred million: Nu yīk + (01-9999999)

Examples

123,906, 214 yātyīk yihchīn sāambaak gáusahpmaahn luhkchīn yihbaak yātsahpsei

When a zero or more than one zero appears between two digits, e.g. 20006 (yihmaahn lìhng luhk), the word "lìhng" is used. "lìhng" here does not mean "zero" but has the same function as "and" in English.

4.2.7 "daih" as a prefix

In Cantonese, when "daih" is used as a prefix to cardinal numbers, it turns them into ordinal numbers. "daih-Nu" must be followed by the measure word of the noun.

Daih Nu M (N)

Examples

Daih yāt go hohksāang haih ngóh pàhngyáuh.

Daih yih go yàhn haih Méihgwok yàhn.

Daih sāam bún syū haih ngóhge (syū).

"daihyih" has a special meaning of "another" or "other". In this usage, "daihyih" must be followed by the measure word of the noun.

Daihyih Nu M (N)

Examples

Ngóh yáuh yāt bún Yīngmàhn syū, móuh daihyih bún.

Ngóh gāmyaht m̀dākhàahn heui Sātìhn, daihyih yaht heui hóu m̀hóu a?

Néih m̀jī, yáuh móuh daihyih go (yàhn) jī a?

4.2.8 Questions formed with "nē?"

"…nē?" is a sentence particle meaning "how about".

S1 V O, S2 nē?

Examples

Ngóh hohk Gwóngdūng wá, néih nē?

Ngóh sing Léih, ngóh ge pàhngyáuh sing Chàhn, néih nē?

Ngóh ūkkéi hái Sātìhn, néih ūkkéi nē?

5 Notes on pragmatic knowledge
語用知識注解 yúhyuhng jīsīk jyugáai

5.1 What to say when going out with friends

5.1.1 Welcome greetings in shops
"fūnyìhng gwōnglàhm" is an expression of welcoming used by most shops and stores or host/hostess in restaurants. Literally, "fūnyìhng" means welcome. "Gwōnglàhm" is a polite way to say the "presence of the guests or visitors". "fūnyìhng" is used in most situations for welcoming your guests. You can use "fūnyìhng" or "fūnyìhng néih".

5.1.2 The use of "要 yiu" vs "想要 séung yiu"
" 要 yiu" is used in ordering food or shopping scenarios indicating the object or things you want. " 想要 séung yiu" is the polite form of " 要 yiu", equivalent to "would like".

5.2 Related knowledge

5.2.1 The use of "yáuhdī"
"yáuhdī" sometimes put in front of adjectives to show a mild degree of the adjectives and soften the tone of the sentences.

6 Contextualized speaking practice
情境説話練習 chìhnggíng syutwah lihnjaahp

6.1 Pronunciation Exercises and Situational Topics

6.1.2 Your Chinese friend comes to visit you and you two are walking around the campus. Following is the campus map. Say the names of the names of the places aloud and pay attention to the pronunciation of "a" in various combinations.

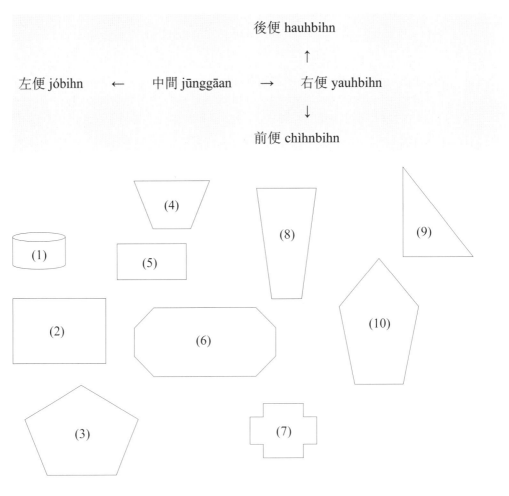

Answer the following questions according to the map above.

根據以上地圖回答問題。Gāngeui yíhseuhng deihtòuh wùihdaap mahntàih.

（1）請問，呢度有冇銀行呀？	Chíngmahn nīdouh yáuh móuh ngàhnhòhng a?
（2）請問，銀行係唔係喺泳池前便呀？	Chíngmahn ngàhnhòhng haihm̀haih hái wihngchìh chìhnbihn a?
（3）請問，呢度有冇書店呀？	Chíngmahn nīdouh yáuhmóuh syūdim a?
（4）請問，宿舍係唔係喺課室後便呀？	Chíngmahn, sūkse haihm̀haih hái fosāt hauhbihn a?
（5）請問，餐廳係唔係喺宿舍旁邊呀？	Chíngmahn, chāantēng haihm̀haih hái sūkse pòhngbīn a?
（6）請問，課室係唔係喺運動場後便呀？	Chíngmahn, fosāt haihm̀haih hái wahnduhng chèuhng hauhbihn a?
（7）你知唔知道超級市場喺邊度呀？	Néih jīm̀jīdou chīukāp síhchèuhng hái bīndouh a?
（8）你知唔知道火車站喺邊度呀？	Néih jīm̀jīdou fóchējaahm hái bīndouh a?

6.1.2　You are going to do exercise at a sports center. You want to make sure you are walking towards the right direction from the bus station. Complete the dialogue according to the map above.

你：請問，嗰度_____呀？	néih: Chíngmahn, gó douh _____ a?
路人：唔_____，嗰度係泳池。	louhyàhn: M _____, gódouh haih wihngchìh.
你：你_____運動場喺邊度呀？	néih: Néih _____ wahnduhng chèuhng hái bīndouh a?
路人：知道，運動場喺_____。	louhyàhn: jīdou, wahnduhng chèuhng hái _____.
你：_____。	néih: _____.

6.1.3 The following is a list of activities people like to do for leisure. Read them aloud and pay attention to the pronunciation.

(1)	野餐	Yéhchāan (picnic)	(2)	寫字	Séjih (Writing characters)
(3)	行街	Hàahnggāai (Window shopping)	(4)	打高爾夫球	Dá gōuyíhfū kàuh (playing golf)
(5)	唱歌	Cheunggō (Karaoke/singing)	(6)	聽音樂	Tēng yāmngohk (listening to music)
(7)	玩風帆	Wáan fūngfàahn (windsurfing)	(8)	探朋友	Taam pàhngyáuh (visiting friends)
(9)	踩單車	Cháai dāanchē (cycling)	(10)	飲茶	Yámchàh (drinking tea)
(11)	飲啤酒	Yám bējáu (drinking beer)	(12)	影相	Yíngséung (taking pictures)

You are going to invite your friend to do something together for fun this weekend.
Tell your classmates what you are going to do. (at least 2 activities)
呢個周末你要同朋友一齊去玩。講俾同學知你地想做乜嘢（至少兩個）。
Nī go jaumuht néih yiu tùhng pàhngyáuh yātchàih heui wáan. Góng béi tùhnghohk jī néihdeih séung jouh mātyéh (ji síu 2 go).

6.1.4 Your Hong Kong friend, Peter, is inviting you to go to watch movies.
你嘅香港朋友 Peter，約你去睇戲。
Néih ge Hēunggóng pàhngyáuh Peter, yeuk néih heui tái hei.

Peter：_____，聽見話呢套電影_____。你_____去睇？	Peter: _____, tēnggin wah nītou dihnyíng _____. Néih _____ heui tái?
你：_____呀，你想_____去睇？	néih: _____ a, néih séung _____ heui tái?
Peter：聽晚，_____？	Peter: Tīngmáahn, _____?
你：聽晚我有事。今晚，_____？	néih: Tīngmáahn ngóh yáuh sih. Gām máahn, _____?

Peter：今晚可以。	Peter: Gāmáan hóyíh.
你：好，噉，我地而家就去。	néih: Hóu, gám ngóhdeih yìhgā jauh heui.
Peter：我想 _____ 先， 然後再去。	Peter: Ngóh séung _____ sīn, yìhnhauh joi heui.
你：好，_____ 見。	néih: Hóu, _____ gin.
Peter：_____ 見。	Peter: _____ gin.

6.1.5 You need to have a group meeting for a project at school. You are discussing the meeting time with your partner. Complete the dialogue according to your schedule.

你嘅時間表 Néih ge sìhgaan bíu (Your schedule)

今日下晝 Gāmyaht hahjau	今晚 Gāmmáahn	聽日上晝 Tīngyaht seuhngjau	聽日下晝 Tīngyaht hahjau	聽晚 tīngmáahn
唔得閒 m̀hdākhàahn	冇嘢做 Móuhyéh jouh	得閒 dākhàahn	唔得閒 m̀hdākhàahn	有嘢做 yáuhyéh jouh
上堂 séuhngtòhng			考試 háausíh	教英文 gaau Yīngmàhn

同學：我地今日下晝見面，好唔好呀？	tùhnghohk: Ngóhdeih gāmyaht hahjau ginmihn, hóum̀hhóu a?
你：今日下晝我要 _____ ， 夜晚冇嘢做。今晚 見，_____ ？	néih: Gāmyaht hahjau ngóh yiu _____ , yehmáahn móuhyéh jouh.Gāmmáahn gin, _____ ?
同學：對唔住，今晚我 _____ 。聽晚 _____ ？	tùhnghohk: Deuim̀hjyuh, gāmmáahn ngóh _____ . Tīngmáahn _____ ?
你：聽晚我要 _____ 。 下晝都 _____ 。 上晝可以。	néih: Tīngmáahn ngóh yiu _____ , Hahjau dōu _____ . Seuhngjau hóyíh.
同學：好，_____ 聽日上晝見。	tùhnghohk: Hóu, _____ tīngyaht seuhngjau gin.

6.2 Speech Topics

1. Chéng néih góng béi ngóhdeih tēng, néih yahtsèuhng sāngwuht ge sìhgaanbíu (timetable).

   請你講俾我哋聽，你日常生活嘅時間表。

   Please tell us the schedule of your daily routine.

2. Chéng néih góng béi ngóhdeih tēng, néih múihyaht hohk Gwóngdūngwá ge sìhgaanbíu.

   請你講俾我哋聽，你每日學廣東話嘅時間表。

   Please tell us your schedule of learning Cantonese.

7. Listening and speaking
聽説練習 tingsyut lihnjaahp

7.1 In the restaurant

安娜：	呢個餸叫乜嘢名呀？	**Ōnnàh:**	Nīgo sung giu mātyéh méng a?
小文：	家常豆腐。	**Síumàhn:**	Gāsèuhng dauhfuh.
安娜：	呢個餸裏邊有冇肉呀？	**Ōnnàh:**	Nīgo sung léuihbihn yáuh móuh yuhk a?
小文：	呢個係齋，冇肉。	**Síumàhn:**	Nīgo haih jāai, móuh yuhk.
安娜：	呢個餸辣唔辣？我唔食辣。	**Ōnnàh:**	Nīgo sung laaht m̀laaht? Ngóh m̀sihk laaht.
小文：	呢個餸有啲辣。噉，我地叫第二個餸啦。	**Síumàhn:**	Nīgo sung yáuh dī laaht. Gám, ngóhdeih giu daihyih go sung lā.
安娜：	我地要一碟炒飯，好唔好呀？	**Ōnnàh:**	Ngóhdeih yiu yātdihp cháaufaahn, hóu m̀hóu a?
小文：	好呀，呢度啲海鮮炒飯好有名。	**Síumàhn:**	Hóu a, nīdouh dī hóisīn cháaufaahn hóu yáuhméng.

Lesson 4　Going out and shopping
行街買嘢

1. Contexts and linguistic functions
語境特徵與語言功能 *yúhgíng dahkjīng yúh yúhyìhn gūngnàhng*

Contexts (who, where, when) 語境特徵（人地時）	Linguistic functions 語言功能
Who: new friends, new acquaintance **Where:** shops, cinema, etc **When:** first few encounter	**Core functions:** Bargaining the price 講價
Language Scenarios: General situations, e.g. in shops, in cinema 一般情況，如商店、電影院	**Supplementary functions:** Asking for general information 取得信息

Notes on pragmatic knowledge	Notes on language structures
I. What to say when shopping or window shopping with friends 　　1. Greeting with "hóu noih móuh gin" 　　2. Greeting with "sihkjó faahn meih a?" II. Related knowledge 　　1. Auxiliary very "hóyíh" and verb particle " dāk" 　　2. Making a request: "béi ngóh táitái"	- Particle "jó" - Questions using "yáuh móuh V" - Adverb: "dōu" - Talking about price and money - The use of "dī" - Reduplication of a verb and the use of "V yāt V", "V háh" - "juhng" as an adverb meaning "also" or "in addition"

2. Texts

課文 fomàhn

2.1 In the classroom

子安：	大衛，食咗飯未呀？	**Jíōn:**	Daaihwaih, sihkjó faahn meih a?
大衛：	仲未（食），而家去食，你呢？	**Daaihwaih:**	Juhng meih (sihk), yìhgā heui sihk, néih nē?
子安：	我都仲未食。	**Jíōn:**	Ngóh dōu juhng meih sihk.
大衛：	一齊去食啦。（你）想去邊度食呀？	**Daaihwaih:**	Yātchàih heui sihk lā. (Néih) séung heui bīndouh sihk a?
子安：	去車站旁邊嗰間餐廳啦，嗰度又平又好食。	**Jíōn:**	Heui chējaahm pòhngbīn gógāan chāantēng lā, gódouh yauh pèhng yauh hóusihk.
大衛：	食完飯，我地去打波，好唔好呀？	**Daaihwaih:**	Sihkyùhn faahn, ngóhdeih heui dábō, hóu m̀hhóu a?
子安：	好呀。	**Jíōn:**	Hóu a.

2.2 On school campus

阿王：	大衛呢？	**A Wóng:**	Daaihwaih nē?
小文：	佢同子安去咗打網球。	**Síumàhn:**	Kéuih tùhng Jíōn heuijó dá móhngkàuh.
阿王：	你知唔知道佢地喺邊度打波呀？	**A Wóng:**	Néih jīm̀jīdou kéuihdeih hái bīndouh dábō a?
小文：	喺體育館旁邊嘅網球場。	**Síumàhn:**	Hái táiyuhk gún pòhngbīn ge móhngkàuh chèuhng.

阿王：	好，唔該你，我而家就去嗰度搵佢。	**A Wóng:**	Hóu, m̀gōi néih, ngóh yìhgā jauh heui gódouh wán kéuih.

2.3　In the classroom

大衛：	小文，噚日你地有冇打波呀？	**Daaihwaih:**	Síumàhn, kàhmyaht néihdeih yáuh móuh dábō a?
小文：	噚日天氣唔好，所以冇打，我地去咗行街。	**Síumàhn:**	Kàhmyaht tīnhei m̀hóu, sóyíh móuh dá, ngóhdeih heuijó hàahnggāai.
大衛：	去咗邊啲地方呀？	**Daaihwaih:**	Heuijó bīndī deihfōng a?
小文：	去咗中環嘅商場。	**Síumàhn:**	Heuijó Jūngwàahnge sēungchèuhng.
大衛：	買咗乜嘢呀？	**Daaihwaih:**	Máaihjó mātyéh a?
小文：	冇買嘢，嗰度啲嘢太貴喇。	**Síumàhn:**	Móuh máaihyéh, gódouh dīyéh taai gwai la.

2.4　In a shop

阿美：	老闆，呢個幾多錢呀？	**A Mēi:**	Lóuhbáan, nīgo géidōchín a?
老闆：	呢個 29 蚊。	**Lóuhbáan:**	Nīgo yihsahp gáu mān.
阿美：	嗰個呢？	**A Mēi:**	Gógo nē?
老闆：	邊個？	**Lóuhbáan:**	Bīngo?
阿美：	就係上便嗰個。	**A Mēi:**	Jauh haih seuhngbihn gógo.
老闆：	嗰個，20 蚊。	**Lóuhbáan:**	Gógo, yihsahp mān.
阿美：	我要嗰個，平啲，得唔得呀？	**A Mēi:**	Ngóh yiu gógo, pèhngdī, dāk m̀dāk a?

老闆：	買兩個嘅話，38 蚊。	**Lóuhbáan:**	Máaih léuhnggo ge wah, sāamsahp baat mān.
阿美：	好，我要兩個。	**A Mēi:**	Hóu, ngóh yiu léuhnggo.

3. Vocabulary in use

活用詞彙 wuhtyuhng chìhwuih

3.1 Common vocabulary

Number	Word	Yale Romanization	POS	English
3.1.1	食咗	sihkjó	PH	have eaten
3.1.2	未	meih	Adv	not yet
3.1.3	仲	juhng	Adv	still
3.1.4	而家	yìhgā	TW	now
3.1.5	都	dōu	Adv	also
3.1.6	一齊	yātchàih	Adv	together
3.1.7	嗰度	gódouh	PW	there
3.1.8	平	pèhng	Adj	cheap
3.1.9	好食	hóu sihk	Adj	good taste
3.1.10	完	yùhn	BF	finish
3.1.11	打波	dábō	V	to play ball
3.1.12	打網球	dá móhngkàuh	V	to play tennis

3.1.13	體育館	táiyuhk gún	PW/N	gymnasium
3.1.14	網球場	móhngkàuh chèuhng	PW/N	tennis court
3.1.15	搵	wán	V	to find; to look for
3.1.16	噖日	kàhmyaht	TW	yesterday
3.1.17	唔好	m̀hóu	PH	not good
3.1.18	行街	hàahnggāai	V	to go window shopping
3.1.19	邊啲地方	bīndī deihfōng	PH	which places
3.1.20	中環	Jūngwàahn	PW	Central
3.1.21	商場	sēungchèuhng	N	shopping mall
3.1.22	買	máaih	V	to buy
3.1.23	啲	dī	M	some
3.1.24	嘢	yéh	N	things
3.1.25	太貴	taai gwai	PH	too expensive
3.1.26	老闆	lóuhbáan	N	boss
3.1.27	幾多錢	géidō chín	PH	how much money
3.1.28	蚊	mān	N	dollar
3.1.29	就係	jauhhaih	Adv	that is
3.1.30	嗰個	gógo	SP	that one
3.1.31	平啲	pèhngdī	PH	cheaper
3.1.32	嘅話	gewah	PH	in case

4 Notes on language structures

語言結構知識 *yúhyìhn gitkau jīsīk*

4.1 Pronunciation guide

Cantonese finals –"a":

Table 4. Cantonese "a" finals

Final Groups	Finals		Key word	English meaning
a	Long	a	sā (沙)	sand
		aai	daai (帶)	bring
		aau	gaau (教)	teach
		aam	sāam (衫)	clothing
		aan	sāan (山)	mountain
		aang	láahng (冷)	cold
		aap	ngaap (鴨)	duck
		aat	baat (八)	eight
		aak	baak (百)	hundred
	Short	ai	dāi (低)	low
		au	gau (夠)	enough
		am	sām (心)	heart
		an	sān (新)	new
		ang	dáng (等)	wait
		ap	sāp (濕)	wet/humid
		at	māt (乜)	what
		ak	dāk (得)	O.K.

There is a distinction between diphthongs having short vowel 'a' (spelt as 'a') and those having long vowel 'a' (spelt as 'aa'). The examples of the long and short "a" are shown in table 5 below:

Table 5. The long and short diphthongs in Cantonese (aai/ai, aam/am, aan/an, aau/au)

	long (aa)		Short (a)	
	Romanization	English	Romanization	English
High level	1. gwāai 2. sāam 3. sāan	good (child) clothing mountain	1. gwāi 2. sām 3. sān	tortoise heart new
High rising	1. gwáai 2. fáan 3. háau	kidnap opposite examination	1. gwái 2. fán 3. háu	ghost powder mouth
Mid level	1. gwaai 2. gaau 3. daai	strange teach take	1. gwai 2. gau 3. dai	expensive enough emperor

4.2 Structure notes

4.2.1 Particle jó

"jó" in Cantonese is usually placed after a verb and indicates action completed.

Examples

Ngóh sihkjó faahn la.

Néihge pàhngyáuh fanjó gaau.

Kéuih gitjó fan (married) la.

4.2.2 Questions using "yáuh móuh V"

Questions using "yáuh móuh V" in Cantonese are similar to "Did you…?" in English.

Examples

Ngóh kàhmyaht m̀dākhàahn, móuh sihkfaahn, móuh fangaau.

Néih yáuh móuh tái nībún syū a? Nībún syū hóu hóutái.

Néihdeih gāmyaht yáuh móuh heui Sātihn a? Gódouh yáuh daaih gáamga (sale) a!

4.2.3 Adverb "都 dōu"

The adverb "都 dōu" sums up the elements that precede it. It comes before the predicate verb and cannot be placed in front of the subject.

Examples

Ngóhge bàhbā, màhmā dōu hóu hóu, yaūhsām, dōjeh néihge gwāansām (concern).

Yīnggwok yàhn, Méihgwok yàhn, Oujāu yàhn, dōu góng Yīngmàhn.

Jūngmàhn syū, Yīngmàhn syū, ngóh dōu séung yiu.

Adverb "dōu" can be used in following structures meaning "also".

S1 Adj/VO, S2 dōu Adj/VO

Examples

Yīnggwok yàhn góng Yīngmàhn, Méihgwok yàhn dōu góng Yīngmàhn.

Sātìhn hóu leng, Jīmsājéui dōu hóu leng.

Léih sīnsāang gaau ngóhdeih, dōu gaau kéuihdeih.

"dōu" can also be used with reduplication of measures of nouns indicating "all of …". It can be used in the subject position.

M M (N) dōu …

Examples

Gogo (yàhn) dōu haih ngóhge pàhngyáuh.

Búnbún syū dōu hóu gwai.

Gāangāan chāantēng ge yéh dōu m̀hóusihk.

4.2.4 Talking about price and money

Dollars and ten cents: Nu mān Nu hòuh

$1.00	→	Yāt mān
$32.00	→	Sāam sahp yih mān
$600.00	→	Luhk baak mān
$1.10	→	Yāt mān yāt hòuh
$10.80	→	Sahp mān baat hòuh
$21.20	→	Yihsahp yāt mān léuhng hòuh
$123.30	→	Yātbaak yihsahp sāam mān sāam hòuh
$2036.70	→	Yihchīn lìhng sāamsahp luhk mān chāt hòuh

$0.10	→	Yāt hòuh
$0.20	→	Léuhng hòuh
$0.50	→	Ńgh hòuh
$3.50	→	Sāam mān ńgh hòuh
$16.50	→	Sahp luhk mān ńgh hòuh

Common form: Nu go Nu

$1.10*	→	Go yāt
$1.20*^	→	Go yih
$1.50*#	→	Go bun
$2.30	→	Léuhnggo sāam
$6.90	→	Luhk go gáu
$12.80	→	Sahpyih go baat
$28.40	→	Yihsahp baat go sei
$132.20^	→	Yātbaak sāamsahp yih go yih
$2532.50#	→	Yihchīn ńgh baak sāamsahp yih go bun

*For $1.10 - $1.9, the first "yāt" (before go) indicating one dollar should be omitted.

^For prices ended with twenty cents, the word "yih" (but not "léuhng") is used.

#For prices ended with fifty cents, the word "bun" (not "ńgh") is used.

4.2.5   The use of "dī"

A lot of adjectives can be used before "dī" to show a comparative degree.

Adj dī

Examples

Nīdī syū hóu gwai, pèhngdī dāk m̀dāk a?

Nīgihn sāam géi hóu, daahnhaih taai sai. Yáuh móuh daaihdī ga?

Nī léuhng go, bīngo lengdī a?

4.2.6 Reduplication of a verb and the use of "V háh"

Using "V háh" indicates that the action is brief or lasts for a short while, e.g. "táiháh" means "take a look".

Example

Ngóh sīngkèih luhk hái ūkkéi táiháh syū, táiháh dihnsih, fanháh gaau; m̀chēutgāai la.

Dáng ngóh táiháh yáuh móuh sìhgaan (time) lā.

Ngóh séung heui Méihgwok, ginháh (see) pàhngyáuh, máaihháh yéh.

4.2.7 "juhng" as an adverb meaning "also" or "in addition"

The adverb "juhng" means "also" or "in addition". It always comes before the verb and it sometimes goes with "tīm", a sentence final particle indicating "more".

S juhng V (O) (tīm)

Examples

Gāmyaht juhng yiu jouh mātyéh a?

Ngóh gāmyaht juhng yiu máaihyéh.

Ngóhdeih kàhmyaht heuijó Sātìhn táihei, máaihyéh, juhng sihkjó hóudō yéh tīm.

5 Notes on pragmatic knowledge

語用知識注解 yúhyuhng jīsīk jyugáai

5.1 What to say when shopping or window shopping with friends

5.1.1 Greeting with "hóu noih móuh gin"

"hóu noih móuh gin" is used to greet someone whom you have not seen for a while. It can also be followed by another greeting, "néih hóu ma?"

5.1.2 Greeting with "sihkjó faahn meih a?"

Greeting with "sihkjó faahn meih a?" is very common in Hong Kong Cantonese. It is a courtesy greeting. While asking the question, the person asking does not have the intention to invite the listener to meal, nor does the person has any intention to get involve in listeners' meal arrangement. It is just a "Hi, how do you do?". Listeners can just answer by saying "sihkjó" (eaten), or "meih sihk" (not yet).

5.2 Related knowledge

5.2.1 Auxiliary verb "hóyíh" and verb particle "-dāk"
Both auxiliary verb "hóyíh" and verb particle "-dāk" mean "can". "hóyíh" can used to refer to the ability, e.g. "ngóh hóyíh sihk hóudō" (I can eat a lot). Both of them are also used in situations that require permission to do something, e.g. "séuhngtòhng sihk m̀sihkdāk yéh a?" or "séuhngtòhng hóm̀hóyíh sihkyéh a? (Can [permission] eat during class?)

"hó m̀hóyíh" can be used to make request, e.g. "ngóh hóm̀hóyíh tùhng néih yātchàih sihkfaahn a?" (Can I eat with you?)

The negatives "m̀hóyíh" and "m̀ (V) dāk" can be used to reject requests.

5.2.2 Making a request, "béi ngóh táitái", "béi ngóh táiháh".
"béi ngóh táitái" is an expression used to request for having a look at something.

Examples
Béi ngóh táitái néih sé (write) mātyéh?
Béi ngóh táitái néih ūkkéi yàhnge séung (photograph) dākm̀dāk a?
M̀gōi néih béi ngóh táiháh, néihge (fēi) gēipiu (air ticket).

6. Contextualized speaking practice
情境説話練習 chìhnggíng syutwah lihnjaahp

6.2 Pronunciation Exercises and Situational Topics

6.2.1 The following is a fast food restaurant menu. Read each item on the menu aloud and pay attention to the pronunciation.

以下係快餐店嘅菜單。請讀出嚟，注意發音。

(1)	雞髀飯套餐	Gāibéi faahn touchāan (chicken leg with rice set)	(2)	魚香肉絲	Yùhhēung yuhksī (Shredded pork in chili sauce)
(3)	素菜餃子	Souchoi gáaují (steamed vegetable dumplings)	(4)	蔥油餅	Chūngyàuh béng (homemade pancake with spring onion)
(5)	海鮮炒飯	Hóisīn cháaufaahn (Fried rice with seafood)	(6)	牛肉炒麵	Ngàuhyuhk cháaumihn (fried noodles with beef)
(7)	上海湯麵	Seuhnghói tōngmihn (noodles with green vegetables in soup)	(8)	糖醋排骨	Tòhngchou pàaihgwāt (Fried spareribs with sweet and sour sauce /sweet-and-sour spareribs))
(9)	雞肉三文治	Gāiyuhk sāammàhnjih (chicken sandwiches)	(10)	火腿三文治	Fótéui sāammàhnjih (ham sandwiches)
(11)	雞扒飯	Gāipá faahn (rice with chicken steak)	(12)	鮮果沙律	Sīngwó sāléut (fruit salad)
(13)	果汁	gwójāp (fruit juice)	(14)	汽水	heiséui (soft drinks)
(15)	奶茶	náaihchàh (milk tea)	(16)	啤酒	bējáu (beer)

6.2.2 Complete the following dialogues in the context of the situation described below.

You are making an order at a fastfood restaurant.

你喺一間快餐店買晏晝。請完成以下對話。

服務員：歡迎光臨。你要乜嘢呢？	Waiter: Fūnyìhng gwōnglàhm. Néih yiu mātyéh nē?

你：我 _____ 。	néih: Ngóh _____ .
服務員：對唔住，_____ 賣晒喇。	Waiter: Deuimjyuh, _____ maaihsaai la.
你：噉，你地有冇 _____ ？	néih: Gám, néihdeih yáuh móuh _____ ?
服務員：有。	Waiter: Yáuh.
你：好，要一個。	néih: Hóu, yiu yātgo.
服務員：好，要 _____ 乜嘢？咖啡 _____ 奶茶？	Waiter: Hóu, yiu _____ mātyéh? Gafē _____ náaihchàh?
你：要 _____ 。	néih: Yiu _____ .
服務員：要熱定凍㗎？	Waiter: Yiu yiht dihng duhng ga?
你：要 _____ 。	néih: Yiu _____ .
服務員：好，請你 _____ 。	Waiter: Hóu, chíng néih _____ .

6.2.3 Today is your friend, Anna's birthday. You want to treat herChinese meal.
Now you are seated in a restaurant.
今日係你朋友安娜生日，你請佢食飯。你地而家喺餐廳點菜。

安娜：多謝你 _____ 。	Ōnnàh: Dōjeh néih _____ .
你：今日係你嘅生日丫嘛。你想唔想 _____ 呀？呢個係呢度最 _____ 嘅菜。	Néih: Gāmyaht haih néih ge sāangyaht āmáh! Néih séung mséung _____ a? Nīgo haih nīdouh jeui _____ ge choi.
安娜：呢個菜 _____ ？	Ōnnàh: Nīgo choi _____ ?
你：呢個菜叫魚香肉絲。	Néih: Nīgo choi giu yùhhēung yuhksī.
安娜：係魚？	Ōnnàh: Haih yú?
你：唔係，係肉。	Néih: Mhaih, haih yuhk.

安娜：係 _____ 肉？ 肉、牛肉 _____ 豬肉？	Ōnnàh: Haih _____ yuhk? Gāiyuhk, ngàuhyuhk _____ jyūyuhk?
你：係豬肉。你 _____？	Néih: Haih jyūyuhk. Néih _____?
安娜：食，我 _____ 都 食。	Ōnnàh: Sihk, ngóh _____ dōu sihk.
你：呢個菜有 _____ 辣。 你可唔可以食 _____？	Néih: Nīgo choi yáuh _____ laaht. Néih hóm̀hóyíh sihk _____?
安娜：可以。	Ōnnàh: Hóyíh.
你：好，噉，我地就 _____ 一個呢個。	Néih: Hóu, gám, ngóhdeih jauh _____ yātgo nīgo.

6.3 Speech Topics

1. Seuhnggo láihbaaiyaht néih tùhng pàhngyáuh heui yātgāan baakfo gūngsī máaihyéh. Gāmyaht néih góngbéi néihge tùhnghohk tēng néihdeih máaihjó dī mātyéh, gódī yéh gwai m̀gwai, géidō chín tùhng leng m̀leng.

上個禮拜日你同朋友去一間百貨公司買嘢。今日你講俾你嘅同學聽你哋買咗啲乜嘢，嗰啲嘢貴唔貴，幾多錢同靚唔靚。

You went shopping with a friend in a department store last Sunday. Today you tell your classmates what you bought, whether those commodities are expensive or pretty and how much they cost.

2. Néihge Méihgwok pàhngyáuh meih heuigwo Hēunggóng ge gāaisíh. Néih góngbéi kéuih tēng gāaisíh yáuh síufáan maaih sāanggwó, tùhng kéuihdeih maaih dī mātyéh sāanggwó. Néih dōu góngbéi kéuih tēng Hēunggóng sāanggwó ge gachìhn tùhng néih jūngyi sihk bīndī sāanggwó.

你嘅美國朋友未去過香港嘅街市。你講俾佢聽街市有小販賣生果，同佢哋賣啲乜嘢生果。你都講俾佢聽香港生果嘅價錢同你鐘意食邊啲生果。

Your American friend has never been to a Hong Kong wet market. You tell him that there are hawkers selling fruits in the market and what fruits they sell. You also tell him about the prices of the fruits and what fruits you like to eat.

7. Listening and speaking

聽說練習 tingsyut lihnjaahp

7.1 On school campus

子安：	好耐冇見，你去咗邊度呀？	**Jíōn:**	Hóu noih móuh gin, néih heuijó bīndouh a?
大衛：	我去咗中國大陸旅行。	**Daaihwaih:**	Ngóh heuijó Jūnggwok daaihluhk léuihhàhng.
子安：	你去咗邊啲地方？有冇去北京呀？	**Jíōn:**	Néih heuijó bīndī deihfōng? Yáuh móuh heui Bākgīng a?
大衛：	冇呀，我去咗上海同廣州，冇去北京。	**Daaihwaih:**	Móuh a, ngóh heuijó Seuhnghói tùhng Gwóngjāu, móuh heui Bākgīng.
子安：	你覺得好玩嗎？	**Jíōn:**	Néih gokdāk hóuwáan ma?
大衛：	好好玩。食咗好多好好食嘅嘢。	**Daaihwaih:**	Hóu hóuwáan. Sihkjó hóudō hóu hóusihk ge yéh.

7.2 In the dormitory

阿美：	你返嚟罅？	**A Mēi:**	Néih fāanlàih làh?
安娜：	返嚟喇。癐死我喇。	**Ōnnàh:**	Fāanlàih la. Guih séi ngóh la.
阿美：	嘩！你買咗好多嘢。買咗乜嘢呀？	**A Mēi:**	Wa! Néih máaihjó hóudō yéh. Máaihjó mātyéh a?
安娜：	我買咗一個手機。	**Ōnnàh:**	Ngóh máaihjó yātgo sáugēi.
阿美：	俾我睇睇。呢個要幾多錢？	**A Mēi:**	Béi ngóh táitái. Nīgo yiu géidōchín?
安娜：	1450 蚊，平唔平呀？	**Ōnnàh:**	Yātchīn sei baak nghsahp mān, pèhng m̀pèhng a?

阿美:	真係好平。仲買咗乜嘢？	**A Mēi:**	Jānhaih hóupèhng. Juhng máaihjó mātyéh?
安娜:	仲買咗三件衫同兩對波鞋。	**Ōnnàh:**	Juhng máaihjó sāam gihn sāam tùhng léuhngdeui bōhàaih.
阿美:	呢對波鞋，好靚呀，我都想去買一對。	**A Mēi:**	Nīdeui bōhàaih, hóu leng a, ngóh dōu séung heui máaih yātdeui.

Lesson 5 Making dinner arrangements
約人食飯

1. Contexts and linguistic functions
語境特徵與語言功能 *yúhgíng dahkjīng yúh yúhyìhn gūngnàhng*

Contexts (who, where, when) 語境特徵 (人地時)	Linguistic functions 語言功能
Who: new friends, new acquaintance, **Where:** on the phone, in the library, etc **When:** first few encounters	**Core functions:** Leaving messages 留言
Language Scenarios: General situations, e.g. on the phone, in library 一般情況，如在電話上、在圖書館	**Supplementary functions:** Enquiring 查詢

Notes on pragmatic knowledge	Notes on language structures

I. How to make an appointment (informal)
  1. See you then: "dou sìh gin"
II. Related knowledge
  1. Asking for agreement: "dím a?"
	- Time When (TW)
	- Clock time
	- Timespent
	- Verb particle "-gán"
	- The verb "béi"
	- Co-verb "béi"

2. Texts
課文 fomàhn

2.1 At the ticket office of a theme park

大衛：	請問迪士尼嘅飛幾多錢呀？	Daaihwaih:	Chíngmahn Dihksihnèihge fēi géidōchín a?
售票員：	一張 550 蚊。你要幾多張呀？	Sauhpiu yùhn:	Yātjēung ńghbaak ńghsahp mān. Néih yiu géidō jēung a?
大衛：	我要兩張。學生有冇平啲呀？	Daaihwaih:	Ngóh yiu léuhngjēung. Hohksāang yáuhmóuh pèhngdī a?
售票員：	冇喎，學生冇優惠。一共 1100 蚊。	Sauhpiu yùhn:	Móuh wo, hohksāang móuh yāuwaih. Yātguhng yātchīn yātbaak mān.
大衛：	可唔可以用信用卡呀？	Daaihwaih:	Hóm̀hóyíh yuhng seunyuhng kāat a?
售票員：	可以。	Sauhpiu yùhn:	Hóyíh.
大衛：	好，請你等一等。呢張係我嘅卡。	Daaihwaih:	Hóu, chíng néih dáng yāt dáng. Nījēung haih ngóhge kāat.

2.2 In the classroom

安娜：	子安，我地邊日去小文屋企呀？	Ōnnàh:	Jíōn, ngóhdeih bīnyaht heui Síumàhn ūkkéi a?
子安：	二月六號，星期四。	Jíōn:	Yih yuht luhk houh, sīngkèih sei.
安娜：	嗰日我有考試。	Ōnnàh:	Góyaht ngóh yáuh háausíh.
子安：	你幾點考完試？	Jíōn:	Néih géidím háauyùhn síh?

安娜：	四點半。	**Ōnnàh:**	Seidím bun.
子安：	噉，冇問題，我地七點之前到佢屋企就得喇。	**Jíōn:**	Gám, móuh mahntàih, ngóhdeih chāatdím jīchìhn dou kéuih ūkkéi jauh dāk la.
安娜：	我地喺邊度等呀？	**Ōnnàh:**	Ngóhdeih hái bīndouh dáng a?
子安：	喺大學圖書館前便等，好唔好呀？	**Jíōn:**	Hái daaihhohk tòuhsyū gún chìhnbihn dáng, hóu m̀hóu a?
安娜：	好，我地幾點見面呀？	**Ōnnàh:**	Hóu, ngóhdeih géidím ginmihn a?
子安：	下晝六點，得唔得呀？	**Jíōn:**	Hahjau luhkdím, dāk m̀dāk a?
安娜：	好，到時見。	**Ōnnàh:**	Hóu, dousìh gin.

2.3 Over the phone

小文：	喂，安娜，我係小文。	Síumàhn:	Wái, Ōnnàh, ngóh haih Síumàhn.
安娜：	你好，小文。	Ōnnàh:	Néih hóu, Síumàhn.
小文：	我地想幫你地開一個歡送會，我想知道你星期幾得閒？	Síumàhn:	Ngóhdeih séung bōng néihdeih hōi yātgo fūnsung wúi, ngóh séung jīdou néih sīngkèih géi dākhàahn.
安娜：	我星期一到星期三晚都得閒。	Ōnnàh:	Ngóh sīngkèih yāt dou sīngkèih sāam máahn dōu dākhàahn.
小文：	好，我地定咗時間之後，再講俾你知啦。	Síumàhn:	Hóu, ngóhdeih dihngjó sìhgaan jīhauh, joi góng béi néih jī lā.
安娜：	好。唔該你。	Ōnnàh:	Hóu. m̀gōi néih.

小文打電話俾子安約佢去歡送會			Síumàhn dá dihnwá béi Jíon yeuk kéuih heui fūnsung wúi.	

子安：	你好，我唔得閒聽你嘅電話。請你喺"咇"一聲之後留言。	**Jíon:**	Néih hóu, ngóh m̀dākhàahn tēng néihge dihnwá. Chíng néih hái "bīt" yātsēng jīhauh làuhyìhn.
小文：	我地幫安娜開一個歡送會，我想知道你下個星期三得唔得閒。你有時間就打電話俾我啦。唔該。	**Síumàhn:**	Ngóhdeih bōng Ōnnàh hōi yātgo fūnsung wúi, ngóh séung jīdou néih hahgo sīngkèih sāam dāk m̀dākhàahn. Néih yáuh sìhgaan jauh dá dihnwá béi ngóh lā. m̀gōi.

3 Vocabulary in use

活用詞彙 wuhtyuhng chìhwuih

3.1 Common vocabulary

Number	Word	Yale Romanization	POS	English
3.1.1	迪士尼	Dihksihnèih	PW	Disneyland
3.1.2	飛（張）	fēi (jēung)	N	ticket
3.1.3	優惠	yāuwaih	N	discount
3.1.4	一共	yātguhng	Adv	in total
3.1.5	可以	hóyíh	AV	can, permitted to, able to
3.1.6	用	yuhng	V	to use
3.1.7	信用卡（張）	seunyuhng kāat (jēung)	N	credit card
3.1.8	等一等	dáng yāt dáng	PH	wait for a while
3.1.9	卡	kāat	N	card
3.1.10	邊日	bīnyaht	PH	which date
3.1.11	屋企	ūkkéi	PW/N	home

3.1.12	二月六號	yih yuht luhk houh	PH	6th February
3.1.13	星期四	sīngkèih sei	TW	Thursday
3.1.14	嗰日	góyaht	TW	that day
3.1.15	幾點	géidím	PH	what time
3.1.16	四點半	sei dím bun	PH	half past four
3.1.17	之前	jīchìhn	Adv	before
3.1.18	到	dou	V	to arrive
3.1.19	見面	ginmihn	V	to meet
3.1.20	到時見	dou sìh gin	PH	see you then
3.1.21	幫	bōng	V	to help
3.1.22	開	hōi	V	to open
3.1.23	歡送會	fūnsung wúi	N	farewell party
3.1.24	星期幾	sīngkèih géi	PH	which day of the week
3.1.25	得閒	dākhàahn	PH	be free
3.1.26	定時間	dihng sìhgaan	PH	set a time
3.1.27	之後	jīhauh	Adv	after
3.1.28	講俾你知	góng béi néih jī	PH	tell you
3.1.29	留言	làuhyìhn	VO	to leave message

4 Notes on language structures

語言結構知識 yúhyìhn gitkau jīsīk

4.1 Pronunciation guide

Cantonese finals (con't)–"e"&"i", "o", "u", "yu"&"eu":

These six vowels are single vowels. When single vowel sounds have no following consonant, they are supposedly pronounced as "long vowels", for example, "mā", "mē", "mī", "mō", "mū".

Table 6. Cantonese single vowels

Final Groups	Finals		Key word	English meaning
e	Long	e	jē(遮)	umbrella
	eng		leng(靓)	beautiful
	ek		tek(踢)	kick
	Short		sei(四)	four
	ei			
i	Long	i	jí(紙)	paper
	iu		bīu(錶)	watch
	im		tìhm(甜)	sweet
	in		tīn(天)	sky
	ip		dihp(碟)	dish
	it		jit(節)	festival
	Short	ing	sing(姓)	surname
	ik		sihk(食)	eat
o	Long	o	ngoh(餓)	hungry
	oi		ngoi(愛)	love
	on		hon(看)	look
	ong		tōng(湯)	soup
	ot		hot(渴)	thirsty
	ok		gwok(國)	country
	Short	ou	chou(醋)	vinegar
u	Long	u	fú(苦)	bitter
	ui		múi(妹)	younger sister
	un		muhn(悶)	boring
	ut		fut(闊)	wide
	Short	ung	tung(痛)	pain
	uk		jūk(粥)	porridge
yu	Long	yu	syū(書)	book
	yun		yùhn(完)	finish
	yut		hyut(血)	blood

The final "eu", "eung", "euk", "eui", "eun" and "eut" are front rounded vowels. For examples, "hēu" (boot); "sēut" (shirt); "seun" (letter); "heui" (to go); "lèuhng" (cool) and "yeuhk" (medicine).

Table 7. Cantonese "eu" finals

Final Groups	Finals		Key word	English meaning
eu	Long	eu	hēu (靴)	boot
	eung		lèuhng (涼)	cool
	euk		jeuk (着)	wear
	Short	eui	heui (去)	go
	eun		seun (信)	letter
	eut		chēut (出)	go out

4.2 Structure notes

4.2.1 Time When (TW)

Time When (TW) denotes a specific point on the time line. In Cantonese, TW includes clock time, dates, day of the week, etc. TW expressions are placed before or right after the subject of a sentence.

(TW) S (TW) V O

Examples

Ngóh gāmyaht sāamdím yiu Séuhngtòhng (attend class).

Néih gāmmáahn baatdím dāk m̀dākhàahn a? Yātchàih táihei hóu m̀hóu a?

Tīngjīu sahpdím ngóh yiu dádihnwá béi màhmā.

4.2.2 Clock time

Time when

4.2.2.1 Nu + dím (Nu o'clock)

Two o'clock	→	Léuhng dím
Four o'clock	→	Sei dím

7:00am	→	Seuhngjau chāt dím
12:00noon	→	Ngaanjau sahpyih dím
6:00pm	→	Hahjau luhk dím
10:00pm	→	Yehmáahn sahp dím
12:00 midnight	→	Bunyé sahpyih dím

4.2.2.2 Nu + dím + Nu

Nu + dím + Nu (1-11) go jih
Nu + dím + Nu (1-59) fān

2:05	Léuhng dím yāt	Léuhng dím yātgo jih	Léuhng dím lìhng ńgh fān
3:10	Sāam dím yih	Sāam dím léuhnggo jih	Sāam dím sahp fān
6:45	Luhk dím gáu	Luhk dím gáugo jih	Luhk dím seisahp ńgh fān
7:55	Chāt dím sahpyāt	Chāt dím sahpyātgo jih	Chāt dím ńghsahp ńgh fān
9:15	Gáu dím sāam	Gáu dím sāamgo jih	Gáu dím sahpńgh fān
11:48	---	---	Sahpyāt dím seisahp baat fān
12:02	---	---	Sahpyih dím lìhng yih fān

4.2.2.3 Half an hour

Nu + dím bun
Nu + dím sāamsahp fān

| 6:30 | Luhk dím bun | Luhk dím sāamsahp fān |
| 12:30 | Sahpyih dím bun | Sahpyih dím sāamsahp fān |

4.2.3 Time spent:

Hour: Nu + go jūng(tàuh)

Bun go jūng(tàuh)	0.5 hour
Yātgo jūng(tàuh)	1 hour
(yāt) gobun jūng(tàuh)	1.5 hour
Léuhnggo jūng(tàuh)	2 hours
Seigo bun jūng(tàuh)	4.5 hour
Sahpsei go jūng(tàuh)	14 hours

Five-minute-period: Nu + go jih

Yātgo jih	5 minutes
Léuhnggo jih	10 minutes
Seigo jih	20 minutes
Gáugo jih	45 minutes

Minute: Nu + fānjūng

Yāt fānjūng	1 minute
Léuhng fānjūng	2 minutes
Sahpyih fānjūng	12 minutes
Sāamsahp fānjūng	30 minutes

4.2.4 Verb particle "-gán"

In Cantonese, "gán" is a verb suffix indicating that an action is, was or will be in progress. It is similar to the continous "be V-ing" in English.

S V-gán O
S haihm̀haih V-gán O
S m̀haih V-gán O
Examples
Néih yìhgā jouhgán mātyéh a?
Ngóh hái chàhlàuh sihkgán faahn.
Néihge pàhngyáuh haihm̀haih hohkgán Gwóngdūng wá a?

Ṁhaih, kéuih hohkgán Yīngmàhn.

4.2.5 The verb "béi"

The word "béi" means "to give". When "béi" is used, the direct object immediately follows "béi", and then the indirect object (the recipient) follows the direct object. In Cantonese, the word order is always as below:

S béi O Person

Examples

Kéuih béi láihmaht (gift) kéuih taaitáai.

Tīngyaht néihge pàhngyáuh sāangyaht, néih béi mātyéh kéuih a?

Ngóh séung béi yātgo daahngōu kéuih.

4.2.6 Co-verb "béi"

The word "béi" can be used as co-verb with verb like "máaih", "maaih", etc.

S V O béi Person

Examples

Ngóhge màhmā máaihjó yātgihn sāam béi ngóh bàhbā.

Néih heuijó Yahtbún (Japan) léuihhàhng, néih máaihjó mātyéh sáuseun (souvenir) béi ūkkéi yàhn a?

Ngóh meih gau sahpbaat seui. Chīukāp síhchèuhng (super market) ṁmaaih jáu (wine) béi ngóh.

The word "béi" can be used to introduce another verb related to the first verb in a sentence

S V1(O) béi Person V2

Examples

Ngóh gāmmáahn jyúfaahn béi néih sihk. Néih séung sihk mātyéh a?

Néih pàhngyáuh sāangyaht, néih hóṁhóyíh cheung sāangyaht gō béi kéuih tēng a?

Ṁgōi néih góng béi ngóh jī néihge dihnwáhouhmáh (number).

5 Notes on pragmatic knowledge

語用知識注解 yúhyuhng jīsīk jyugáai

5.1 How to make an appointment (informal)

5.1.1. See you then: "dou sìh gin"

"dou sìh gin" is used frequently to end the conversation when arranging a meeting with friends or expecting to meet someone in a certain time.

Examples

A: Hah sīngkèih yātchàih sihkfaahn, hóuṁhóu a?

B: Hóu a! Sīngkèih géi a? Hái bīndouh sihk a?

A: Sīngkèih sei máahn, dākṁdāk a? Ngóhdeih heui sihk jihjohchāan (buffet), hóuṁhóu a?

B: Hóu a! ngóh sīngkèih sei yehmáahn chātdím jīhauh dākhàahn.

A: Hóu! Gám, ngóh dehng chāt dím bun lā.

B: Hóu a! Dousìh gìn.

5.2 Related knowledge

5.2.1. Asking for agreement: "dím a?"

"dím a?" has the same meaning as "hóuṁhóu a?" and functions as a question tag to ask for agreement.

Examples

Hóu noih móuh gin, néih dím a?

Tēng gin wah (I heard that) néih behngjó hóu noih, néih yìhgā dím a?

Yānwaih tòihfūng, néih pàhngyáuhge fēigēi chìhjó dou Hēunggóng. Néih jī mjī néih pàhngyáuh yìhgā dím a?

6. Contextualized speaking practice

情境説話練習 chìhnggíng syutwah lihnjaahp

6.1 Pronunciation Exercises and Situational Topics

6.1.1 The following are the names of cities in China. Listen and read them aloud.

（1）	北京	Bākgīng (Beijing)	（2）	廣州	Gwóngjāu (Guangzhou)
（3）	海南	Hóinàahm (Haninan)	（4）	海口	Hóiháu (Haikou)
（5）	武漢	Móuhhon (Wuhan)	（6）	青島	Chīngdóu (Qingdao)
（7）	上海	Seuhnghói (Shanghai)	（8）	哈爾濱	Hāyíhbān (Haerbin)

Léih táai and Lisa are talking about Chinese New Year plans. Please read aloud.

李太：	麗莎，你咁鍾意香港，你幾時請你爸爸同媽媽嚟香港玩呀？	Léih táai:	Laihsā, néih gam jūngyi Hēunggóng, néih géisìh chéng néih bàhbā tùhng màhmā làih Hēunggóng wáan a?
麗莎：	我爸爸同媽媽打算中國新年嚟香港玩。	Laihsā:	Ngóh bàhbā tùhng màhmā dásyun Jūnggwok sānnìhn làih Hēunggóng wáan.
李太：	新年嚟香港最好玩。中國新年有好多好食嘅嘢，學校都放假，你可以帶佢哋去好多地方玩。	Léih táai:	Sānnìhn làih Hēunggóng jeui hóuwáan. Jūnggwok sānnìhn yáuh hóudō hóusihk ge yéh, hohkhaauh dōu fongga, néih hóyíh daai kéuihdeih heui hóudō deihfōng wáan.
麗莎：	我本來想喺放假嗰陣時，去中國旅行，而家爸爸同媽媽新年要嚟，所以今年聖誕節，我一放假就去中國。	Laihsā:	Ngóh búnlòih séung hái fongga gójahnsìh, heui Jūnggwok léuihhàhng, yìhgā bàhbā tùhng màhmā sānnìhn yiu làih, sóyíh gāmnìhn Singdaanjit, ngóh yāt fongga jauh heui Jūnggwok.

李太：	你想去中國邊度玩呀？	**Léih táai:**	Néih séung heui Jūnggwok bīndouh wáan a?
麗莎：	好多人話桂林好靚。我有一個好鍾意旅行嘅朋友住喺桂林，所以我一放假就會同幾個同學一齊去桂林玩，同埋探佢。中國新年會留喺香港陪家人。	**Laihsā:**	Hóudō yàhn wah Gwailàhm hóu leng. Ngóh yáuh yātgo hóu jūngyi léuihhàhng ge pàhngyáuh jyuhhái Gwailàhm, sóyíh ngóh yāt fongga jauh wúih tùhng géigo tùhnghohk yātchàih heui Gwailàhm wáan, tùhngmàaih taam kéuih. Jūnggwok sānnìhn wúih làuhhái Hēunggóng pùih gāyàhn.

6.2 Speech Topics

1. Chéng néih góngbéi ngóhdeih tēng, seuhnggo láihbaai néih jouhjó mātyéh.
   請你講俾我哋聽，上個禮拜你做咗乜嘢。
   Please tell us what you have done last week.

2. Chéng néih góngháh néih fongga gójahnsìh jūngyi jouh mātyéh.
   請你講吓你放假嗰陣時鍾意做乜嘢。
   Please tell us what you like to do during your holiday.

7. Listening and speaking
聽說練習 tingsyut lihnjaahp

7.1 In the library

小文：	準備考試嘎?!	**Síumàhn:**	Jéunbeih háausíh àh?!
大衛：	唔係，我寫緊一個報告。	**Daaihwaih:**	M̀haih, ngóh ségán yātgo bougou.
小文：	學期結束之後，你想做乜嘢呀？	**Síumàhn:**	Hohkkèih gitchūk jīhauh, néih séung jouh mātyéh a?

大衛：	我要去中國大陸旅行，之後返美國。	**Daaihwaih:**	Ngóh yiu heui Jūnggwok daaihluhk léuihhàhng, jīhauh fāan Méihgwok.
小文：	你去旅行之前，我地一齊食飯啦。	**Síumàhn:**	Néih heui léuihhàhng jīchìhn, ngóhdeih yātchàih sihkfaahn lā.
大衛：	好呀，下星期我考完試之後打電話俾你啦。	**Daaihwaih:**	Hóu a, hah sīngkèih ngóh háauyùhn síh jīhauh dádihnwá béi néih lā.
小文：	好，我等你電話。你繼續寫報告啦，我走先。	**Síumàhn:**	Hóu, ngóh dáng néih dihnwá. Néih gaijuhk sé bougou lā, ngóh jáu sīn.
大衛：	好，遲啲見。	**Daaihwaih:**	Hóu, chìhdī gin.

Mid-term Review L1-L5

1. Review on Cantonese pronunciation:

There are fifty-one syllable endings in real life Cantonese vocabulary.

Table 8. 51 "Finals" in Cantonese

L	S	L	S	L	S	L	S	L	S	L	S	L
a		e		eu		i		o		u		yu
aai	ai		ei		eui			oi		ui		
aau	au					iu			ou			
aam	am					im						
aan	an				eun	in		on		un		yun
aang	ang	eng		eung			ing	ong			ung	
aap	ap					ip						
aat	at				eut	it		ot		ut		yut
aak	ak	ek		euk			ik	ok			uk	

Note: L = long, S = short

2. You are chatting casually with your friends. Some of them ask you questions, please answer the following questions.

1. Néihdeih jūng m̀jūngyi hohk Gwóngdūngwá a?

_____

2. Gó léuhnggo hohksāang haihm̀haih Yahtbún yàhn a?

_____

3. Nītìuh chèuhng fu hóu leng, géidōchín a? Hái bīndouh máaih a?

_____

4. Ngóhdeih tīngyaht géidímjūng heui yámchàh a?

_____

5. Néih géiyuht géihouh sāangyaht a?

_____

6. Néih sāangyaht, néih pàhngyáuh máaih mātyéh béi néih a?

_____

3. Provide the questions appropriate to the following answers.

1. Q:

_____

A: Ngóh haih Méihgwok yàhn, m̀haih Yīnggwok yàhn. Ngóh taaitáai dōu haih Méihgwok yàhn.

2. Q:

_____

A: Ngóh jūngyi nībún syū, m̀jūngyi góbún.

3. Q:

_____

A: Ngóh baatdím bun fāanhohk, seidím bun fonghohk.

4. Q:

_____

A: Cháangm̀gwai, sahpmān seigo.

5. Q:

_____

A: Yātnìhn yáuh sāambaak luhksahp ńgh yaht.

6. Q:

_____

A: Ngóh béi yātbún Gwóngdūngwá syū gógo hohksāang.

4. Texts

課文 fomàhn

In the classroom

李先生：	早晨，你哋好嗎？	**Léih sīnsāang:**	Jóusàhn, néihdeih hóu ma?
學生：	好，你呢？	**Hohksāang:**	Hóu, néih nē?
李先生：	我都幾好。今日我哋有幾個新（嘅）同學。佢係瑪麗，佢係保羅，佢係王先生。王先生係英國華僑。保羅係美國人。瑪麗係加拿大人。佢哋都學廣東話。	**Léih sīnsāang:**	Ngóh dōu géi hóu. Gāmyaht ngóhdeih yáuh géigo sān(ge) tùhnghohk. Kéuih haih Máhlaih, kéuih haih Bóulòh, kéuih haih Wòhng sīnsāang. Wòhng sīnsāang haih Yīnggwok wàhkìuh. Bóulòh haih Méihgwok yàhn. Máhlaih haih Gānàhdaaih yàhn. Kéuihdeih dōu hohk Gwóngdūngwá.
保羅、瑪麗、王先生：	你哋好。	**Bóulòh, Máhlaih, Wòhng sīnsāang:**	Néihdeih hóu.
保羅：	呢班有幾多個學生呀？	**Bóulòh:**	Nībāan yáuh géidō go hohksāang a?
張太：	呢班而家有八個學生。	**Jēung táai:**	Nībāan yìhgā yáuh baatgo hohksāang.
保羅：	你哋鍾唔鍾意學廣東話呀？	**Bóulòh:**	Néihdeih jūng m̀jūngyi hohk Gwóngdūngwá a?
張太：	我哋好鍾意學廣東話，你哋呢？	**Jēung táai:**	Ngóhdeih hóu jūngyi hohk Gwóngdūngwá, néihdeih nē?
保羅、瑪麗、王先生：	我哋都好鍾意學廣東話。你哋學咗幾耐廣東話呀？	**Bóulòh, Máhlaih, Wòhng sīnsāang:**	Ngóhdeih dōu hóu jūngyi hohk Gwóngdūngwá. Néihdeihhohkjó géinoih Gwóngdūngwá a?
張太：	我哋學咗三個月嘑。你哋有冇廣東話書呀？	**Jēung táai:**	Ngóhdeih hohkjó sāamgo yuht la. Néihdeih yáuh móuh Gwóngdūngwá syū a?

保羅、瑪麗、王先生：	我哋冇廣東話書。	**Bóulòh, Máhlaih, Wòhng sīnsāang:**	Ngóhdeih móuh Gwóngdūngwá syū.
李先生：	你哋今日買書啦！	**Léih sīnsāang:**	Néihdeih gāmyaht máaih syū lā!
保羅：	廣東話書貴唔貴呀？幾多錢一本呀？	**Bóulòh:**	Gwóngdūngwá syū gwai m̀gwai a? Géidō chín yātbún a?
李先生：	廣東話書唔係幾貴，一百一十蚊一本。你哋學唔學中國字呀？	**Léih sīnsāang:**	Gwóngdūngwá syū m̀haih géi gwai, yātbaak yātsahp mānyātbún. Néihdeih hohk m̀hohk Jūnggwok jih a?
保羅：	我同瑪麗唔學中國字，王先生學。	**Bóulòh:**	Ngóh tùhng Máhlaih m̀hohk Jūnggwok jih, Wòhng sīnsāang hohk.

Lesson 6 Getting to know new friends
識新朋友

1. Contexts and linguistic functions
語境特徵與語言功能 yúhgíng dahkjīng yúh yúhyìhn gūngnàhng

Contexts (who, where, when) 語境特徵（人地時）	Linguistic functions 語言功能
Who: friends, new acquaintance **Where:** home, friend's home, café, etc **When:** general	**Core functions:** Giving recommendation 推介
Language Scenarios: General situations, e.g. chat with friends 一般情況，如和朋友閒談	**Supplementary functions:** Confirming 確認

Notes on pragmatic knowledge	Notes on language structures

I. How to talk to new acquaintance
  1. Metaphorical use of "deihfōng"
  2. Accepting and refusing politely
II. Related knowledge
  1. Useful expressions to introduce people
  2. Quality assessment with "mdāk"
	- Verb particle "-gwo"
	- Preposition "hái"
	- Auxiliary verb "wúih"
	- The use of "yíhgīng"
	- The use of "gójahn sìh"
	- Manner of action and complement of degree
	- The use of "dō" and "síu" with verbs showing V-more or V-less
	- Aduerb "jauh"

2. Texts

課文 fomàhn

2.1 On school campus

安德：	你好。我叫安德，我係新嚟嘅留學生。	**Ōndāk:**	Néih hóu. Ngóh giu Ōndāk, ngóh haih sān làih ge làuhhohksāang.
阿王：	你好。我叫王子強 Aaron，啲朋友都叫我阿王。	**A Wóng:**	Néih hóu. Ngóh giu Wòhng Jíkèuhng Aaron, dī pàhngyáuh dōu giu ngóh A Wóng.
安德：	阿王，好開心認識你。	**Ōndāk:**	A Wóng, hóu hōisām yíhngsīk néih.
阿王：	我都好開心。呢次係唔係你第一次嚟香港呀？	**A Wóng:**	Ngóh dōu hóu hōisām. Nīchi haih m̀haih néih daih yāt chi làih Hēunggóng a?
安德：	係呀，我以前冇嚟過香港。	**Ōndāk:**	Haih a, ngóh yíhchìhn móuh làihgwo Hēunggóng.
阿王：	噉，有乜嘢要幫手，就搵我，唔使客氣。我嘅手機號碼係 9876543。	**A Wóng:**	Gám, yáuh mātyéh yiu bōngsáu, jauh wán ngóh, m̀sái haakhei. Ngóhge sáugēi houhmáh haih 9876543.
安德：	多謝你。我仲未有香港嘅手機號碼。有，我就講俾你知啦。	**Ōndāk:**	Dōjeh néih. Ngóh juhng meih yáuh Hēunggóngge sáugēi houhmáh. Yáuh, ngóh jauh góng béi néih jī lā.

2.2 In the dormitory

阿王：	返嚟嘞。	**A Wóng:**	Fāanlàih làh.
安德：	阿王，你今日唔使上堂咩？	**Ōndāk:**	A Wóng, Néih gāmyaht m̀sái séuhngtòhng mē?

阿王：	今日冇堂。一陣間我要去機場接我媽媽。	A Wóng:	Gāmyaht móuh tòhng. Yātjahn gāan ngóh yiu heui gēichèuhng jip ngóh màhmā.
安德：	佢喺邊度嚟呀？	Ōndāk:	Kéuih hái bīndouh làih a?
阿王：	佢喺波爾多嚟。	A Wóng:	Kéuih hái Bōyíhdō làih.
安德：	波爾多喺邊度？	Ōndāk:	Bōyíhdō hái bīndouh?
阿王：	喺法國，你知唔知道法國喺邊度呀？	A Wóng:	Hái Faatgwok, néih jīm̀jīdou Faatgwok hái bīndouh a?
安德：	知道，我食過法國菜，法國菜好貴。	Ōndāk:	Jīdou, ngóh sihkgwo Faatgwok choi, Faatgwok choi hóu gwai.
阿王：	你鍾唔鍾意食呀？	A Wóng:	Néih jūngm̀jūngyi sihk a?
安德：	好鍾意。	Ōndāk:	Hóu jūngyi.
阿王：	噉，今晚，我地一齊去食法國菜，好唔好呀？	A Wóng:	Gám, gāmmáahn, ngóhdeih yātchàih heui sihk Faatgwok choi, hóu m̀hóu a?
安德：	好，不過今晚我約咗朋友。	Ōndāk:	Hóu, bātgwo gāmmáahn ngóh yeukjó pàhngyáuh.
阿王：	唔緊要，下次有機會再一齊食啦。	A Wóng:	M̀gányiu, hahchi yáuh gēiwuih joi yātchàih sihk lā.
安德：	好。	Ōndāk:	Hóu.

2.3 In the dormitory

| 安德： | 阿王，你得閒嗰陣時，鍾意做乜嘢呀？ | Ōndāk: | A Wóng, néih dākhàahn gójahnsìh, jūngyi jouh mātyéh a? |
| 阿王： | 我鍾意打波同游水。 | A Wóng: | Ngóh jūngyi dábō tùhng yàuhséui. |

| 安德: | 喺德國，我會去公園畫畫，同朋友傾偈。嚟咗香港之後，讀書比較忙，得閒嗰陣時，就喺宿舍休息。我而家最鍾意學中文。 | Ōndāk: | Hái Dākgwok, ngóh wúih heui gūngyún waahkwá, tùhng pàhngyáuh kīnggái. Làihjó Hēunggóng jīhauh, duhksyū béigaau mòhng, dākhàahn gójahnsìh, jauh hái sūkséh yāusīk. Ngóh yìhgā jeui jūngyi hohk Jūngmàhn. |
| 阿王: | 咁好，我地以後就多啲用中文傾偈啦。 | A Wóng: | Gam hóu, ngóhdeih yíhhauh jauh dōdī yuhng Jūngmàhn kīnggái lā. |

2.4 In a restaurant

子安:	大家好，我嚟介紹一下，呢個係我嘅德國朋友安德。佢識講少少廣東話，請你哋多啲用中文同佢傾偈。	Jíōn:	Daaihgā hóu, ngóh làih gaaisiuh yātháh, nīgo haih ngóhge Dākgwok pàhngyáuh Ōndāk. Kéuih sīk góng síusíu Gwóngdūng wá, chíng néihdeih dōdī yuhng Jūngmàhn tùhng kéuih kīnggái.
安德:	你哋好，我叫安德。好開心認識你哋。	Ōndāk:	Néihdeih hóu, ngóh giu Ōndāk. Hóu hōisām yihngsīk néihdeih.
嘉欣:	安德，你好。我叫嘉欣，我係子安嘅中學同學。	Gāyān:	Ōndāk, néih hóu. Ngóh giu Gāyān, ngóh haih Jíōn ge jūnghohk tùhnghohk.
安德:	你好。你而家仲係學生嘎？	Ōndāk:	Néih hóu. Néih yìhgā juhnghaih hohksāang àh?
嘉欣:	我已經畢咗業喇，而家喺一間美國 IT 公司做嘢。你呢？	Gāyān:	Ngóh yíhgīng bātjó yihp la, yìhgā hái yātgāan Méihgwok IT gūngsī jouhyéh. Néih nē?
安德:	我係留學生，而家喺中文大學，讀國際商業。	Ōndāk:	Ngóh haih làuhhohksāang, yìhgā hái Jūngmàhn daaihhohk, duhk Gwokjai sēungyihp.

3 Vocabulary in use

活用詞彙 wuhtyuhng chìhwuih

3.1 Common vocabulary

Number	Word	Yale Romanization	POS	English
3.1.1	新嚟嘅	sān làih ge	PH	newly come
3.1.2	留學生	làuhhohk sāang	N	study abroad student
3.1.3	朋友	pàhngyáuh	N	friend
3.1.4	開心	hōisām	Adj	happy
3.1.5	認識	yihngsīk	V	to know someone
3.1.6	呢次	nīchi	PH	this time
3.1.7	第一次	daih yāt chi	PH	the first time
3.1.8	嚟	làih	V	to come
3.1.9	過	gwo	BF	experienced
3.1.10	幫手	bōngsáu	V	to help
3.1.11	唔使客氣	m̀sái haakhei	PH	not at all, don't be polite
3.1.12	手機	sáugēi	N	mobile phone
3.1.13	號碼	houhmáh	N	number
3.1.14	返嚟	fāanlàih	V	to come back
3.1.15	機場	gēichèuhng	N	airport
3.1.16	接	jip	V	to meet and pick up
3.1.17	法國菜	Faatgwok choi	N	French cuisine
3.1.18	不過	bātgwo	Adv	however
3.1.19	約	yeuk	V	to make appointment
3.1.20	下次	hahchi	PH	next time
3.1.21	有機會	yáuh gēiwuih	PH	have chance
3.1.22	游水	yàuhséui	V	to swim

3.1.23	畫畫	waahkwá	V	to draw, to paint
3.1.24	同朋友傾偈	tùhng pàhngyáuh kīnggái	PH	to chat with friends
3.1.25	讀書	duhksyū	V	to study
3.1.26	比較	béigaau	Adj	comparatively, relatively
3.1.27	忙	mòhng	Adj	busy
3.1.28	宿舍	sūkse / sūkséh	N	dormitory
3.1.29	休息	yāusīk	V	to rest
3.1.30	以後	yíhhauh	Adv	afterwards
3.1.31	多啲	dōdī	PH	more
3.1.32	大家	daaihgā	N	everyone
3.1.33	少少	síusíu	PH	a little bit
3.1.34	中學	jūnghohk	N	secondary school
3.1.35	畢咗業	bātjóyihp	PH	graduated

3.2 Proper nouns

3.2.1	安德	Ōndāk	Name	On Dak, Andrew
3.2.2	王子強	Wòhng jíkèuhng	Name	Wong Ji Keung
3.2.3	阿王	A Wóng	Name	Aaron
3.2.4	嘉欣	Gāyān	Name	Ga Yan
3.2.5	波爾多	Bōyíhdō	PW	Bordeaux
3.2.6	法國	Faatgwok	PW	France
3.2.7	德國	Dākgwok	PW	Germany
3.2.8	公園	gūngyún	PW/N	public park
3.2.9	國際商業	Gwokjai sēungyihp	N	International Business

4. Notes on language structures
語言結構知識 yúhyìhn gitkau jīsīk

4.1 Structure notes

4.1.1 Verb particle "-gwo"

"gwo" is used to indicate past experience. It can only be used to talk about actions or incidents happened in the past. It can come with sentence-end particle "la" emphasizing a change of status. "meih" or "mouh" can come before "gwo" as in "meih sihk gwo Faatgwok choi" (haven't experienced French cuisine) as a negation. "juhng meih…" can be used to emphasize "still not yet".

S V-gwo O
S meih/móuh V-gwo O
S V-gwo O meih a?

Examples

Néih heuigwo Hóiyèuhng gūngyún (Ocean Park) meih a? Tēn gin wah gódouh hóu hóuwán (fun)!

Ngóh meih heuigwo Hóiyèuhng gūngyún, ngóh heuigwo Dihksihnèih (Disneyland)!

Ngóh pàhngyáuh hohkgwo Faatmàhn (French), kéuih hái Faatgwok jyuhgwo géi nìhn.

Kéuih taaitáai meih hohkgwo jyúfaahn, daahnhaih kéuih jyúge yéh hóu hóusihk.

4.1.2 Preposition "hái"

"hái" can be used to mean "from"

S hái PW heui/làih PW

Examples

Ngóh gāmyaht yiu hái Sātìhn heui Jīmsājéui, dím heui jeui faai (fastest) a?

Néih jīmjī hái Hēunggóng heui Tòihwāan ge gēipiu géidōchín a?

Ngóh bàhbā hah sīngkèih hái Bākgīng làih Hēunggóng gūnggon (business trip).

4.1.3 Auxiliary verb "wúih"

"wúih" in this lesson means something is going to happen. It is similar to "will be" in English.

Examples

Tīngyaht wúih lohkyúh (rain).

Néih behngjó hóu noih la, géisìh wúih hóufāan (get well)a?

Néih yuhng taai noih dihnnóuh, dihnnóuh wúih hóu yiht!

4.1.4 Auxiliary verbs

Common auxiliary verbs in Cantonese include "yiu", "sīk", "séung", "wúih", "hóyíh" and "jūngyi". "m̀" is put in front of the auxiliary verbs to negate the sentence.

S AV V O

Sm̀AV VO

S AV m̀AV V O a?

Examples

Néih sīk m̀sīk góng Gwóngdūng wá a?

Ngóh séung heui Jīmsājéui, chíngmahn néih jīm̀jī dím heui a?

Ngóhm̀hóyíh góng béi néih jī ngóhge sānfánjing (identity card) houhmáh.

Ngóhge pàhngyáuh sìhsìh (often) làih Hēunggóng, daahnhaih kéuihm̀jūngyi heui yámchàh.

Néih hóm̀hóyíh daai (bring) ngóh heui Hóiyèuhng gūngyún a?

The choice-type questions for "hóyíh" and "jūngyi" in modern Cantonese in Hong Kong should be "hóm̀hóyíh … a?" and "jūng m̀jūngyi … a?" respectively.

4.1.5 Verb expression in series "Yuhng N V (O)"

"yuhng" is used before a noun to express the manner in which, the second action is carried out.

Examples

Ngóh yuhng nībún syū hohk Gwóngdūng wá.

M̀hóyíh yuhng nībouh dihnnóuh séuhngmóhng (go online), nībouh dihnnóuh yáuh mahntàih.

Jūnggwok yàhn yuhng faaijí (chopsticks) sihkfaahn, néih sīkm̀sīk yuhng a?

4.1.6 The use of "yíhgīng"

"yíhgīng" means "already" and it is commonly used before a verb phrase and with the verb suffix "-jó". Sentence-end particle "la" can be used at the end of the sentence to emphasize change of status. The negative counterpart is "juhng meih…"

Examples

Néih bàhbā yíhgīng làihjó Hēunggóng. Néih juhngmeih heui gēichèuhng jip (see someone in the airport) kéuih àh?

Ngóh hohkjó hóu noih, juhngmeih hohksīk yàuhséui.

Màhmā yíhgīng jyújó faahn la, néihm̀hóu sihk lihngsihk (snacks) la.

4.1.7 The use of "gójahn sìh"

"gójahn sìh" means "when" and it is used after a verb phrase to indicate that something happened, happens or will happen in a certain period of time.

V gójahn sìh, …

Examples

Ngóhdeih sihkfaahn gójahnsìh yám mātyéh jáu hóu nē?

Néih fangán gaau gójahnsìh yáuh yàhn dá dihnwá béi néih.

Néih heui Yahtbún gójahnsìh hóm̀hóyíh bōng (help) ngóh máaih dī yéh a?

4.1.8 Manner of action and complement of degree

"dāk" is used with an adjective and makes the adjective adverbial showing the manner of action.

V dāk Adj

Examples

Néih hàahngdāk hóu faai, hóm̀hóyíh dáng yāt dáng ngóh a?

Néih jyúfaahn jyúdāk gam hóu sihk, géisìh joi jyú béi ngóhdeih sihk a?

Néih wah bīngo cheunggō chēungdāk jeui hóutēng a?

The degree complement describes the degree or the extent that the action or quality achieved (usually an adjective). Adverb "hóu" or "gam" can precede the complement adjective.

4.1.9 Adverb "jauh" (then)

The adverb "jauh" means "then" and it should be put right before the verb of the second clause.

Examples

Néih yáuh sìhgaan jauh dá dihnwá béi ngóh lā.

Yùhgwó (If) ngóh jīdou, ngóh jauh wah béi néih jī.

Néih háauyùhn síh (finish exam), ngóhdeih jauh yātchàih heui léuihhàhng (travel) lā.

4.1.10 The use of "dō" and "síu" with verbs showing V-more or V-less

This construction is expressing that the action or deed should be done more "dō", or less "síu". You can add numerical unit to the verb to indicate that something is more or less than it originally was.

Examples

Ngóh gau la. Néih sihk dōdī lā.

Néih sāntáiṁhóu, yám síudī jáu lā.

Hohk Gwóngdūng wá yiu góng dōdī.

5. Notes on pragm atic knowledge

語用知識注解 yúhyuhng jīsīk jyugáai

5.1 How to talk to newacquaintance

5.1.1 Metaphorical use of "deihfōng"

"deihfōng" means "place". It can be used in Cantonese to mean a physical location or a part or an aspect of abstract things, e.g. "néih yáuh ṁmìhngbaahk ge deihfōng, jauh yiu mahn ngóh" (you have things you don't understand, you need to ask me).

"bīndouh" literally means "where" in questions asking for location. It can be used metaphorically. "néih yáuh bīndouh ṁmìhngbaahk, jauh yiu mahn ngóh" (you have things you don't understand, you need to ask me).

5.1.2　Accepting and refusing politely

"móuh mahntàih" means "no problem", thus it is a reply accepting invitation or offer.

"deui m̀jyuh, ngóh yáuh yéh jouh" is a polite way to decline an invitation. "yáuh yéh jouh" literally means "have something to do" which shows that there are other engagements.

"m̀gányiu" literally means "not important", however it is used in polite speech to mean "it doesn't matter". It can be used as a polite reply to a rejection.

"hahchi yáuh gēiwuih joi yātchàih V" or in short form "hahchi lā" means "let's do it next time" to close the conversation.

5.2 Related knowledge

5.2.1　Useful expressions to introduce people

"ngóh làih gaaisiuh háh" or "dáng ngóh làih gaaisiuh" are expressions to use when you are doing an introduction to someone or among new friends. "làih" in the expression does not have the directional function.

5.2.2　Quality assessment with "m̀dāk"

"m̀dāk" can mean "no good" and "not capable of doing something". It has a sense of personal assessment as poor quality by the speaker. "meih dāk" means "not yet ok" indicating that something still needs to be improved or needs time to prepare.

6. Contextualized speaking practice

情境説話練習 chìhnggíng syutwah lihnjaahp

6.1 Pronunciation Exercises and Situational topics

Jēung táai and Mary are talking about their hobbies and Saturday plans. Please fill in the missing words and read aloud.

張太：	你放假_____鍾意做乜嘢呀？	Jēung táai:	Néih fongga _____ jūngyi jouh mātyéh a?
瑪麗：	我鍾意飲茶、買嘢、聽音樂、睇書、睇電視_____睇戲。我都鍾意去旅行同做運動。	Máhlaih:	Ngóh jūngyi yámchàh, máaihyéh, tēng yāmngohk, táisyū, tái dihnsih _____ táihei. Ngóh dōu jūngyi heui léuihhàhng tùhng jouh wahnduhng.
張太：	你鍾意做_____運動呀？	Jēung táai:	Néih jūngyi jouh _____ wahnduhng a?
瑪麗：	我鍾意打網球、打籃球、同_____單車等等。	Máhlaih:	Ngóh jūngyi dá móhngkàuh, dá làahmkàuh, tùhng _____ dāanchē dángdáng.
張太：	我都想做運動。我哋下個禮拜六_____游水，好唔好呀？	Jēung táai:	Ngóh dōu séung jouh wahnduhng. Ngóhdeih hahgo láihbaai luhk _____ yàuhséui, hóu m̀hóu a?
瑪麗：	好……但係……我唔_____游水。	Máhlaih:	Hóu …… daahnhaih…… ngóh m̀ _____ yàuhséui.
張太：	唔緊要，我可以教你。	Jēung táai:	M̀gányiu, ngóh hóyíh gaau néih.

Jēung táai is inviting Mary to go to dimsum, please fill in the missing words and read aloud.

張太：	瑪麗，你聽日得唔得閒呀？	Jēung táai:	Máhlaih, néih tīngyaht dāk m̀dākhàahn a?
瑪麗：	有_____事呀？	Máhlaih:	Yáuh _____ sih a?
張太：	我嘅朋友李太叫我哋一齊去飲茶。你得唔得閒呀？佢_____俾我聽有一間茶樓嘅點心好好食。你可以食叉燒包，蝦餃，燒賣，同春卷……等等。我都會_____我啲新嘅朋友俾你識。	Jēung táai:	Ngóhge pàhngyáuh Léih táai giu ngóhdeih yātchàih heui yámchàh. Néih dāk m̀dākhàahn a? Kéuih ____ béi ngóh tēng yáuh yātgāan chàhlàuh ge dímsām hóu hóusihk. Néih hóyíh sihk chāsīubāau, hāgáau, sīumáai tùhng chēun gyún…… dángdáng. Ngóh dōu wúih _____ ngóh dīsānge pàhngyáuh béi néih sīk.

瑪麗：	好呀！我下個禮拜，每日上晝都要學廣東話，但係下晝好 _____ 。我都好想飲茶。	**Máhlaih:**	Hóu a! Ngóh hahgo láihbaai múihyaht seuhngjau dōu yiu hohk Gwóngdūngwá, daahnhaih hahjau hóu _____. Ngóh dōu hóu séung yámchàh.
張太：	好。我 _____ 俾我朋友聽先，請佢訂枱。我遲啲打電話俾你，講俾你 _____ 我哋幾點飲茶啦。	**Jēung táai:**	Hóu. Ngóh _____ béi ngóh pàhngyáuh teng sīn, chéng kéuih dehng tói. Ngóh chìhdī dá dihnwá béi néih, góngbéi néih _____ ngóhdeih géidím yámchàh lā.

6.2 Speech Topics

1. Chéng gaaisiuhháh néihge gāyàhn tùhng kéuihdeih jūngyi jouh mātyéh.

   請介紹吓你嘅家人同佢地鍾意做乜嘢。

   Please give a brief introduction to the class about your family and tell us what they like to do most.

2. Chàhn táai giu néih heui yámchàh, néih séung giu dō yātgo pàhngyáuh. Yìhgā néih dá dihnwá chéng néih pàhngyáuh làih, tùhngmàaih góngháh néih jūngyi sihk mātyéh dímsām.

   陳太叫你去飲茶，你想叫多一個朋友。而家你打電話請你朋友嚟，同埋講吓你鍾意食乜嘢點心。

   Mrs. Chan invites you to have dimsum, and would you like to bring one more friend. Now you call your friend to come and talk with him/her which dimsum you like to eat.

7. Listening and speaking
聽說練習 tingsyut lihnjaahp

7.1 On school campus

德華：	安德，你嚟咗香港幾耐呀？	Dākwàh:	Ōndāk, néih làihjó Hēunggóng géinoih a?
安德：	我嚟咗兩個星期喇。	Ōndāk:	Ngóh làihjó léuhnggo sīngkèih la.

德華：	你嘅廣東話講得好好。	Dākwàh:	Néihge Gwóngdūng wá góngdāk hóu hóu.
安德：	邊度係呀，我仲學緊，講得麻麻地。	Ōndāk:	Bīndouh haih a, ngóh juhng hohkgán, góngdāk màhmádéi.
德華：	你學咗幾耐呀？	Dākwàh:	Néih hohkjó géinoih a?
安德：	我喺德國學咗一年半普通話同中文，而家學緊廣東話，學咗兩個星期。	Ōndāk:	Ngóh hái Dākgwok hohkjó yātnìhn bun Póutūngwá tùhng Jūngmàhn, yìhgā hohkgán Gwóngdūng wá, hohkjó léuhnggo sīngkèih.
德華：	學咗一年半中文。嘩，好犀利呀。學咗兩個星期就講得咁好，你學得好快呀！	Dākwàh:	Hohkjó yātnìhn bun Jūngmàhn. Wa, hóu sāileih a. Hohkjó léuhnggo sīngkèih jauh góngdāk gam hóu, néih hohkdāk hóu faai a!
安德：	唔得，我嘅聲調仲未得，時時講錯。	Ōndāk:	M̀dāk, ngóhge sīngdiuh juhng meih dāk, sìhsìh góngcho.
德華：	練習多啲就得啦。	Dākwàh:	Lihnjaahp dōdī jauh dāk lā.

7.2 At Dākwah's home

德華：	安德，請你入嚟。呢個係我細佬德寶。	Dākwàh:	Ōndāk, chéng néih yahplàih. Nīgo haih ngóh sailóu Dākbóu.
德寶：	你好，安德，歡迎你。	Dākbóu:	Néih hóu, Ōndāk, fūnyìhng néih.
安德：	德寶，你好。	Ōndāk:	Dākbóu, néih hóu.
德寶：	安德，請坐。要唔要飲啲嘢？果汁，汽水定係啤酒呀？	Dākbóu:	Ōndāk, chíng chóh. Yiu m̀yiu yámdik yéh? Gwójāp, heiséui dihnghaih bējáu a?
安德：	我飲啤酒啦。唔該。聽德華講，你好鍾意做運動。	Ōndāk:	Ngóh yám bējáu lā. M̀gōi. Tēng Dākwàh góng, néih hóu jūngyi jouh wahnduhng.
德寶：	係呀，游水，打波，跑步，跳舞，我都鍾意。	Dākbóu:	Haih a, yàuhséui, dábō, páaubouh, tiumóuh, ngóh dōu jūngyi.

安德：	你打乜嘢波呀？	**Ōndāk:**	Néih dá mātyéh bō a?
德寶：	我時時打籃球，有時打乒乓波，而家學緊打網球。	**Dākbóu:**	Ngóh sìhsìh dá làahmkàuh, yáuhsìh dá bīngbām bō, yìhgā hohkgán dá móhngkàuh.
安德：	你鍾意打網球嗄，得閒，我地可以一齊打。	**Ōndāk:**	Néih jūngyi dá móhngkàuh àh, dākhàahn, ngóhdeih hóyíh yātchàih dá.
德寶：	我學咗冇幾耐，打得唔好。	**Dākbóu:**	Ngóh hohkjó móuh géi noih, dádāk m̀hóu.
安德：	唔緊要，我都打得麻麻地。	**Ōndāk:**	M̀gányiu, ngóh dōu dádāk màhmádéi.

Lesson 7 Seeking advice from medical doctor
約見醫生

1. Contexts and linguistic functions
語境特徵與語言功能 yúhgíng dahkjīng yúh yúhyìhn gūngnàhng

Contexts (who, where, when) 語境特徵（人地時）	Linguistic functions 語言功能
Who: friends, new acquaintance, **Where:** in restaurants, friend's home, etc **When:** general	**Core functions:** Describing 描述
Language Scenarios: General situations, e.g. in restaurants, chat with friends 一般情況，如在餐廳、和朋友閒談	**Supplementary functions:** Telling the way 指路

Notes on pragmatic knowledge	Notes on language structures

I. How to make reservations (semi-formal) and leave a message
   1. Confirming with "haih mhaih a?"
   2. Phone calss: calling and receiving
   3. Making reservations
II. Related knowledge
   1. Polite way to request people to do things for you: "màhfàahn néih"
	- Adverb "dōu"
	- Preposition "離 lèih"
	- Questions word "dím"/"dímyéung"
	- Sentence-end particles in Cantonese

2. Asking questions with "dímgáai" and "jouh mātyéh"
3. Offering, accepting and refusing help politely

2. Texts

課文 fomàhn

2. In the classroom

安娜：	呢次係我第一次嚟香港，一定要試下廣東點心。	**Ōnnàh:**	Nīchi haih ngóh daihyāt chi làih Hēunggóng, yātdihng yiu siháh Gwóngdūng dímsām.
安德：	我去過一間好地道嘅茶樓，叫明星茶樓。	**Ōndāk:**	Ngóh heuigwo yātgāan hóu deihdouhge chàhlàuh, giu Mìhngsīng chàhlàuh.
安娜：	嗰度嘅點心，種類多唔多？	**Ōnnàh:**	Gódouhge dímsām, júngleuih dōmdō?
安德：	種類好多，而且都好好食，仲有，佢地嘅服務都好好。	**Ōndāk:**	Júngleuih hóudō, yìhché dōu hóu hóusihk, juhngyáuh, kéuihdeihge fuhkmouh dōu hóu hóu.
安娜：	貴唔貴呀？	**Ōnnàh:**	Gwai m̀gwai a?
安德：	我唔記得喇，一個人一百蚊左右啦。	**Ōndāk:**	Ngóh m̀geidāk la, yātgo yàhn yātbaak mān jóyáu lā.
安娜：	嗰間茶樓喺邊度呀？離呢度遠唔遠呀？	**Ōnnàh:**	Gógāan chàhlàuh hái bīndouh a? Lèih nīdouh yúhnm̀yúhn a?
安德：	唔遠。	**Ōndāk:**	M̀yúhn.

安娜：	喺呢度點樣去呀？	Ōnnàh:	Hái nīdouh dímyéung heui a?
安德：	喺呢度，坐火車去，坐兩個站，就到喇。	Ōndāk:	Hái nīdouh, chóh fóchē heui, chóh léuhnggo jaahm, jauh dou laak.

2.2 Over the phone

安德：	喂，德華，我係安德。	Ōndāk:	Wái, Dākwàh, ngóh haih Ōndāk.
德華：	安德，你好。搵我有乜嘢事呀？	Dākwàh:	Ōndāk, néih hóu. Wán ngóh yáuh mātyéh sih a?
安德：	聽日中午得唔得閒呀？我同嘉欣想約你同德寶食飯。	Ōndāk:	Tīngyaht jūngngh dāk m̀dākhàahn a? Ngóh tùhng Gāyān séung yeuk néih tùhng Dākbóu sihkfaahn.
德華：	好呀，喺邊度食呀？	Dākwàh:	Hóu a, hái bīndouh sihk a?
安德：	我地想去明星茶樓。你知唔知道喺邊度呀？	Ōndāk:	Ngóhdeih séung heui Mìhngsīng chàhlàuh. Néih jīm̀jīdou hái bīndouh a?
德華：	我諗我知道，係唔係喺九龍公園附近呀？	Dākwàh:	Ngóh nám ngóh jīdou, haih m̀haih hái Gáulùhng gūngyún fuhgahn a?
安德：	係呀，就喺九龍公園對面。	Ōndāk:	Haih a, jauh hái Gáulùhng gūngyún deuimihn.
德華：	好，知道喇。聽日中午幾點呢？	Dākwàh:	Hóu, jīdou laak. Tīngyaht jūngngh géidím nē?
安德：	中午十二點半，得唔得呀？	Ōndāk:	Jūngngh sahpyih dím bun, dākm̀dāk a?
德華：	好，冇問題。訂咗位未呀？	Dākwàh:	Hóu, móuh mahntàih. Dehngjó wái meih a?
安德：	已經訂咗喇，訂咗安先生，四位。	Ōndāk:	Yíhgīng dehngjó la, dehngjó Ōn sīnsāang, sei wái.
德華：	好。聽日見。	Dākwàh:	Hóu. Tīngyaht gin.

2.3 In the dormitory

阿王：	安德，你點解仲唔起身呀？係唔係唔舒服呀？	A Wóng:	Ōndāk, néih dímgáai juhng m̀héisān a? haih m̀haih m̀syūfuhk a?
安德：	係呀，我諗我病咗。	Ōndāk:	Haih a, ngóh nám ngóh behngjó.
阿王：	你邊度唔舒服呀？	A Wóng:	Néih bīndouh m̀syūfuhk a?
安德：	頭痛，我覺得我發燒。肚都有啲唔舒服。	Ōndāk:	Tàuhtung, ngóh gokdāk ngóh faatsīu. Tóuh dōu yáuhdī m̀syūfuhk.
阿王：	你想唔想去睇醫生呀？	A Wóng:	Néih séung m̀séung heui tái yīsāng a?
安德：	我而家唔想去，我想休息一下。	Ōndāk:	Ngóh yìhgā m̀séung heui, ngóh séung yāusīk yātháh.
阿王：	好，噉，你休息一陣，我去上堂先。	A Wóng:	Hóu, gám, néih yāusīk yātjahn, ngóh heui séuhngtòhng sīn.
安德：	你返黎嗰陣時，可唔可以幫幫我，你可唔可以買啲嘢俾我食呀？	Ōndāk:	Néih fāanlàih gójahnsìh, hóm̀hóyíh bōngbōng ngóh, néih hóm̀hóyíh máaih dī yéh béi ngóh sihk a?
阿王：	冇問題，你想食乜嘢呀？	A Wóng:	Móuh mahntàih, néih séung sihk mātyéh a?
安德：	餅乾或者麵包都得。	Ōndāk:	Bénggōn waahkjé mihnbāau dōu dāk.

2.4 Over the phone

德華：	安德，你而家喺邊度呀？	Dākwàh:	Ōndāk, néih yìhgā hái bīndouh a?
安德：	我而家喺屋企休息。	Ōndāk:	Ngóh yìhgā hái ūkkéi yāusīk.
德華：	聽講你噚日入咗醫院，你點呀？	Dākwàh:	Tēnggóng néih kàhmyaht yahpjó yīyún, néih dim a?
安德：	我冇留院，不過我喺醫院急症室等咗一晚。	Ōndāk:	Ngóh móuh làuh yún, bātgwo ngóh hái yīyún gāpjing sāt dángjó yātmáahn.

德華：	乜嘢事呀？	**Dākwàh:**	Mātyéh sih a?
安德：	前晚我忽然胃痛，痛得好犀利，所以就去醫院急症室。	**Ōndāk:**	Chìhnmáahn ngóh fātyìhn waihtung, tungdāk hóu sāileih, sóyíh jauh heui yīyún gāpjing sāt.
德華：	你點樣去醫院？	**Dākwàh:**	Néih dímyéung heui yīyún?
安德：	我朋友送我去。	**Ōndāk:**	Ngóh pàhngyáuh sung ngóh heui.
德華：	噉，你知唔知道點解胃痛呢？	**Dākwàh:**	Gám, néih jīmjīdou dímgáai waih tung nē?
安德：	醫生話大概係感冒，護士同我打咗針，仲俾咗啲藥我，之後就叫我返屋企喇。	**Ōndāk:**	Yīsāng wah daaihkoi haih gámmouh, wuhsih tùhng ngóh dájó jām, juhng béijó dī yeuhk ngóh, jīhauh jauh giu ngóh fāan ūkkéi laak.
德華：	噉，你點解喺醫院等咗一晚呢？	**Dākwàh:**	Gám, néih dímgáai hái yīyún dángjó yātmáahn nē?
安德：	因為病嘅人太多，所以我喺嗰度等咗好耐。	**Ōndāk:**	Yānwaih behngge yàhn taai dō, sóyíh ngóh hái gódouh dángjó hóu noih.

3. Vocabulary in use

活用詞彙 wuhtyuhng chìhwuih

3.1 Common vocabulary

Number	Word	Yale Romanization	POS	English
3.1.1	試	si	V	to try
3.1.2	點心	dímsām	N	dimsum
3.1.3	地道	deihdouh	Adj	with local taste

3.1.4	茶樓	chàhlàuh	N	tea house
3.1.5	種類	júngleuih	N	type, kind
3.1.6	而且	yìhché	Adv	furthermore
3.1.7	服務	fuhkmouh	N	service
3.1.8	唔記得	m̀geidāk	PH	forgot
3.1.9	左右	jóyáu	Adv	approximately
3.1.10	離	lèih	Adv	apart
3.1.11	遠	yúhn	Adj	far
3.1.12	點樣	dímyéung	QW	how
3.1.13	坐	chóh	V	to sit, to take vehicle
3.1.14	中午	jūngngh	TW	noon
3.1.15	諗	nám	V	to think
3.1.16	附近	fuhgahn	TW	nearby
3.1.17	對面	deuimihn	TW	opposite to
3.1.18	訂位	dehngwái	V	to make reservation
3.1.19	點解	dímgáai	QW	why
3.1.20	起身	héisān	V	to wake up
3.1.21	唔舒服	m̀syūfuhk	PH	not feeling well
3.1.22	病咗	behngjó	PH	be sick
3.1.23	頭痛	tàuhtung	N	headache
3.1.24	發燒	faatsīu	V	to have fever
3.1.25	肚	tóuh	N	belly
3.1.26	睇醫生	tái yīsāng	V	to see doctor
3.1.27	餅乾	bénggōn	N	biscuits
3.1.28	或者	waahkjé	Adv	or, maybe
3.1.29	麵包	mihnbāau	N	bread
3.1.30	入咗醫院	yahpjó yīyún	PH	to be hospitalized

3.1.31	留院	làuhyún	V	to stay in hospital
3.1.32	胃痛	waihtung	N	stomachache
3.1.33	犀利	sāileih	Adj	serious
3.1.34	送	sung	V	to send
3.1.35	大概	daaihkoi	Adv	about, approximately
3.1.36	感冒	gámmouh	N	flu
3.1.37	打咗針	dájó jām	Ph	injected
3.1.38	藥	yeuhk	N	medicine

3.2 Proper nouns

3.2.1	德華	Dākwàh	Name	Dak Wa
3.2.2	德寶	Dākbóu	Name	Dak Bou
3.2.3	明星茶樓	Mìhngsīng chàhlàuh	Name	Ming Sing tea house
3.2.4	九龍公園	Gáulùhng gūngyún	PW	Kowloon Park
3.2.5	護士	wuhsih	N	nurse
3.2.6	急症室	gāpjing sāt	PW/N	emergency unit (hospital)

4. Notes on language structures
語言結構知識 yúhyìhn gitkau jīsīk

4.1 Structure notes

4.1.1 Adverb "dōu": inclusiveness and exclusiveness

"Question word … dōu…" is a construction used to indicate inclusive ideas such as "everything" and "anything".

Examples

Ngóh gāmyaht behngjó, mātyèh dōu m̀séung sihk.

Heui bīndouh sihkfaahn dōu dāk, néih kyutdihng (decide) lā.

Ngóh bàhbā hóu mòhng, géisìh dōum̀dākhàahn.

4.1.2 Preposition "離 lèih"

"Lèih" is used to express degree of distance in space and showing the distance only, as in "PW1 lèih PW2 yúhnm̀yúhn a?" (Is PW1 far from PW2?). "hái" meaning "from" is a right word to use if movement is involved, as in "ngóh hái PW1 heui PW2" (I go from PW1 to PW2).

4.1.3 Asking and giving direction

"dímyéung heui PW" and "dím heui PW" are constructions asking directions. The construction literally means "how to go to PW".

Examples

Chíngmahn dímyéung heui Sātìhn fóchē jaahm a?

Hái nīdouh dím heui Jīmsājéui a? Yiu daap mātyéh chē a?

Ngóh séung heui Ngòhlòhsī (Russia), néih jīm̀jī dím heui a?

4.1.4 Questions word "dím"/"dímyéung"

"dímyéung" or its short form "dím" can be used before verbs, meaning "how to V", as in "dímyéung góng a?" (how to say?)

"dím a?" can be used as a question tag, which has similar function as "hóum̀hóu a?" or "dākm̀dāk a?" as in "tīngyaht yātchàih heui chàhlàuh sihkfaahn, dím a?" (Tomorrow we go together to Chinese teahouse to eat, what do you think?)

4.1.5 Sentence-end particles in Cantonese

There are a number of sentence-end particles in Cantonese as shown by research in Cantonese linguistics. Sentence-end particles are put at the end of a sentence. Each sentence-end particle has its own linguistics and/or pragmatic functions, for example, "a?" is a questioning particle used in choice-type and wh-questions, "tìm" emphasizes "more", "la" shows change in status, "àh?" uses for reconfirmation, "lā" shows suggestions, etc.

5. Notes on pragmatic knowledge
語用知識注解 yúhyuhng jīsīk jyugáai

5.1 How to make reservations (semi-formal) and leave a message

5.1.1 Confirming with "haih m̀haih a?"
In a context where someone is already certain about something, "haih m̀haiha?" can be used to seek further confirmation.

5.1.2 Phone calls: calling and receiving
"wái" is a common greeting when receiving phone calls. You can ask, "chíngmahn (néih) wán bīnwái a?"for work domain or "(néih) wán bīngo a?" in casual settings.

"wán ngóh yáuh mātyéh sih a?" is asking "what is the matter?""Chíngmahn…" can be added to the phrase in formal settings, such as in work domain.

5.1.3 Making reservations
"ngóh séung dehngwái" literally means "I want to reserve a seat/a place" and the phrase can be used for making reservations. "wái" literally means "seat". You can use "ngóh séung dehng tói" for "I want to reserve a table" and "ngóh séung dehng fóng" for "I want to reserve a room", etc.

5.2 Related knowledge

5.2.1 Polite way to request people to do things for you, "màhfàahn néih…"
"màhfàahn néih" is used to request for help. It can be used before verb phrases, such as in "Màhfàahn néih máaih dī yéh béi ngóh sihk" (I would trouble you to buy something for me to eat). "Màhfàahn saai (néih)" can be used to thank someone for the help.

5.2.2 Asking questions with "dímgáai" and "jouh māt"
Both "dímgáai" and "jouh māt" can be used to enquire for reasons, causes or purposes. "dímgáai" means "why". "jouh māt" is used in casual settings, normally with friends. "jouh māt" can also be used to express disagreement and enquire for a reason, e.g. "jouh māt néih m̀sihkfaahn a?" (why don't you eat?).

5.2.3　Offering, accepting and refusing help politely

You can offer help to someone by asking "sái m̀sái bōng néih…" (would you like me to help by…). "m̀sái màhfàahn néih" (no need to trouble you) can be used as polite way to decline the offer for help. "m̀sái" (no need) is a short form and is used in casual settings.

6. Contextualized speaking practice

情境說話練習 chìhnggíng syutwah lihnjaahp

6.1　Pronounication Exercises and Situational Topics

Gālèuhng is not feeling well and he visits his doctor. Please read aloud.

醫生：	陳家良，你邊度唔舒服呀？	**Yīsāng:**	Chàhn Gālèuhng, néih bīndouh m̀syūfuhk a?
家良：	兩三個星期前，我有少少發燒，流鼻水，有時有啲暈，因為當時我好忙，冇時間睇醫生。我去藥房買咗啲藥水，我食咗啲藥，覺得好啲，但係兩個星期前開始咳，咳到而家。	**Gālèuhng:**	Léuhng sāam go sīngkèih chìhn, ngóh yáuh síusíu faatsīu, làuh beihséui, yáuhsìh yáuhdī wàhn, yānwaih dōngsìh ngóh hóu mòhng, móuh sìhgaan tái yīsāng. ngóh heui yeuhkfòhng máaihjó dī yeuhkséui, ngóh sihkjó dī yeuhk, gokdāk hóudī, daahnhaih lèuhng go sīngkèih chìhn hōichín kāt, kātdou yìhgā.
醫生：	你除咗咳之外，而家仲有冇唔舒服呀？有冇胃口呀？瞓唔瞓得呀？	**yīsāng:**	Néih chèuihjó kāt jīngoih, yìhgā juhng yáuh móuh m̀syūfuhk a? Yáuh móuh waihháu a? Fan m̀fandāk a?
家良：	我胃口都幾好，但係晚晚瞓唔着，因為夜晚一瞓喺度就咳。	**Gālèuhng:**	Ngóh waihháu dōu géi hóu, daahnhaih máahnmáahn fan m̀jeuhk, yānwaih yehmáahn yāt fan hái douh jauh kāt.
醫生：	噉，你而家仲有冇鼻水同痰呀？	**Yīsāng:**	Gám, néih yìhgā juhng yáuh móuh beihséui tùhng tàahm a?

家良：	我而家好似冇鼻水，但係有好多痰，咳得好辛苦。	**Gālèuhng:**	Ngóh yìhgā hóuchíh móuh beihséui, daahnhaih yáuh hóudō tàahm, kātdāk hóu sānfú.
醫生：	我俾呢啲藥你食，睇吓可唔可以止咳，同埋，因為你咳咗咁耐，你都約一個時間照 X-光，睇吓有冇問題，如果有問題你再嚟見我啦。	**Yīsāng:**	Ngóh béi nīdī yeuhk néih sihk, táiháh hómhóyíh jíkāt, tùhngmàaih, yānwaih néih kātjó gam noih, néih dōu yeuk yātgo sìhgaan jiu īksìh-gwōng, táiháh yáuh móuh mahntàih, yùhgwó yáuh mahntàih néih joi làih gin ngóh lā.
家良：	好啦，唔該晒你。	**Gālèuhng:**	Hóu lā, m̀gōisaai néih.

6.2 Speech Topics

1. Chàhn sīnsāang dá dihnwá wán néihge pàhngyáuh, daahnhaih kéuihm̀hái douh. Chéng néih góng béi Chàhn sīnsāang tēng.

   陳先生打電話搵你嘅朋友，但係佢唔喺度。請你講俾陳先生聽。

   Mr. Chan called you to look for your friend, but he/she is not with you. Please tell Mr. Chan.

2. Néih m̀syūfuhk heui tái yīsāng. Chíng néih góng béi yīsāng jī néih bīndouh m̀syūfuhk tùhng yáuh mātyéh mahntàih.

   你唔舒服去睇醫生，請你講俾醫生知你邊度唔舒服同有乜嘢問題。

   You are not feeling well and go to see doctor. Please tell your doctor which part of your body is not well and what is the issue.

7. Listening and speaking

聽説練習 tingsyut lihnjaahp

7.1 In a restaurant

| 服務員： | 請問，飲乜嘢茶？ | **Fuhkmouh yùhn:** | Chíngmahn, yám mātyéh chàh? |

安德：	你地決定啦。我乜嘢茶都飲。	**Ōndāk:**	Néihdeih kyutdihng lā. Ngóh mātyéh chàh dōu yám.
德華：	嘉欣，你想飲乜嘢茶呀？	**Dākwàh:**	Gāyān, néih séung yám mātyéh chàh a?
嘉欣：	我識紅茶同綠茶，第二啲都唔識。	**Gāyān:**	Ngóh sīk hùhngchàh tùhng luhkchàh, daihyih dī dōu m̀sīk.
德華：	噉，我地飲香片啦。	**Dākwàh:**	Gám, ngóhdeih yám hēungpín lā.
嘉欣：	好。安德，你最鍾意食乜嘢呀？	**Gāyān:**	Hóu. Ōndāk, néih jeui jūngyi sihk mātyéh a?
安德：	我最鍾意食叉燒包同春卷。	**Ōndāk:**	Ngóh jeui jūngyi sihk chāsīubāau tùhng chēun gyún.
德華：	你呢，你要乜嘢呀？	**Dākwàh:**	Néih nē, néih yiu mātyéh a?
嘉欣：	我要蝦餃同燒賣。	**Gāyān:**	Ngóh yiu hāgáau tùhng sīumáai.
德華：	好。伙記，呢張係我地嘅點心紙，唔該你。	**Dākwàh:**	Hóu. Fógei, nījēung haih ngóhdeihge dímsām jí, m̀gōi néih.

7.2　On the street

安德：	阿王，呢度附近有冇藥房呀？	**Ōndāk:**	A Wóng, nīdouh fuhgahn yáuh móuh yeuhkfòhng a?
阿王：	車站附近有好多藥房。	**A Wóng:**	Chējaahm fuhgahn yáuh hóudō yeuhkfòhng.
安德：	邊間藥房比較好呀？	**Ōndāk:**	Bīngāan yeuhkfòhng béigaau hóu a?
阿王：	我時時去嗰間喺商場旁邊，使唔使我陪你去呀？	**A Wóng:**	Ngóh sìhsìh heui gógāan hái sēungchèuhng pòhngbīn, sái m̀sái ngóh pùih néih heui a?
安德：	唔使麻煩你喇，講俾我知點樣去，就得喇。	**Ōndāk:**	M̀sái màhfàahn néih la, góng béi ngóh jī dímyéung heui, jauh dāk la.
阿王：	喺車站出嚟之後，轉左，藥房喺商場左邊。	**A Wóng:**	Hái chējaahm chēutlàih jīhauh, jyunjó, yeuhkfòhng hái sēungchèuhng jóbihn.

Lesson 8 Talking about holidays
傾下假期

1. Contexts and linguistic functions
語境特徵與語言功能 yúhgíng dahkjīng yúh yúhyìhn gūngnàhng

Contexts (who, where, when) 語境特徵（人地時）	Linguistic functions 語言功能
Who: friends, new acquaintance **Where:** in travel agent, café, etc **When:** general	**Core functions:** Explaining 説明
Language Scenarios: General situations, e.g. chat with friends, travel agents 一般情況，如和朋友閒談、旅行社 Talking about travel plans 計劃旅行	**Supplementary functions:** Comparing 比較

Notes on pragmatic knowledge	Notes on language structures
I. How to find travel companion 　1. Making decision 　2. Introducing a different topic II. Related knowledge 　1. Making a choice with "dihnghaih"	- Verb-object (VO) structure - Comparative constructions - "waahkjé" and "dihnghaih" - The usage of "tùhng" and "yātchàih" - "chóh" as a co-verb telling means of transportation - Resultative verb "dóu"

2. Texts

課文 fomàhn

2.1 In the dormitory

安德：	阿王，放假嗰陣時，你有乜嘢打算呀？	Ōndāk:	A Wóng, fongga gójahnsìh, néih yáuh mātyéh dásyun a?
阿王：	七月，我會去英國。	A Wóng:	Chātyuht, ngóh wúih heui Yīnggwok.
安德：	去英國邊度呀？	Ōndāk:	Heui Yīnggwok bīndouh a?
阿王：	去倫敦，參加一個學校活動，然後喺嗰度玩幾日。	A Wóng:	Heui Lèuhndēun, chāamgā yātgo hohkhaauh wuhtduhng, yìhnhauh hái gódouh wáan géiyaht.
安德：	我三年前去過倫敦。夏天去倫敦幾好，夏天倫敦天氣涼過香港好多。	Ōndāk:	Ngóh sāam nìhn chìhn heuigwo Lèuhndēun. Hahtīn heui Lèuhndēun géihóu, hahtīn Lèuhndēun tīnhei lèuhnggwo Hēunggóng hóudō.
阿王：	我知道倫敦有好多值得睇嘅歷史建築。	A Wóng:	Ngóh jīdou Lèuhndēun yáuh hóudō jihkdāk táige lihksí ginjūk.
安德：	係呀。如果你鍾意睇自然風景，仲可以去南部海岸玩下。	Ōndāk:	Haih a. Yùhgwó néih jūngyi tái jihyìhn fūnggíng, juhng hóyíh heui nàahmbouh hóingohn wáanháh.
阿王：	我邊度都想去，不過仲要睇我嘅錢夠唔夠。係喇，我聽日要去辦簽證。	A Wóng:	Ngóh bīndouh dōu séung heui, bātgwo juhng yiu tái ngóhge chín gau m̀gau. Haih laak, ngóh tīngyaht yiu heui baahn chīmjing.
安德：	辦簽證麻唔麻煩呀？	Ōndāk:	Baahn chīmjing màh m̀màhfàahn a?
阿王：	幾麻煩，要填表，影相，仲要準備證明文件，而且仲要俾錢。	A Wóng:	Géi màhfàahn, yiu tìhnbíu, yíngséung, juhng yiu jéunbeih jingmìhng màhngín, yìhché juhngyiu béichín.

2.2 On the street

安德：	對唔住，我想問下，世界大樓係唔係喺附近呀？	Ōndāk:	Deui m̀jyuh, ngóh séung mahnháh, Saigaai Daaihlàuh haih m̀haih hái fuhgahn a?
路人：	係呀，離呢度唔遠，就喺前便，你睇唔睇到展覽中心呀？	Louhyàhn:	Haih a, lèih nīdouh m̀yúhn, jauh hái chìhnbihn, néih tái m̀táidóu Jínláahm jūngsām a?
安德：	睇到。	Ōndāk:	Táidóu.
路人：	你向嗰個方向行，過咗前便嗰個路口，轉左，就睇到喇。	Louhyàhn:	Néih heung gógo fōngheung hàahng, gwojó chìhnbihn gógo louhháu, jyunjó, jauh táidóu la.
安德：	唔該晒。	Ōndāk:	M̀gōi saai.

3. Vocabulary in use
活用詞彙 wuhtyuhng chìhwuih

3.1 Common vocabulary

Number	Word	Yale Romanization	POS	English
3.1.1	放假	fongga	V	to have vacation
3.1.2	打算	dásyun	V/N	to plan, plan
3.1.3	學校活動	hohkhaauh wuhtduhng	N	school activities
3.1.4	然後	yìhnhauh	Adv	then, afterwards
3.1.5	三年前	sāam nìhn chìhn	PH	three years ago
3.1.6	夏天	hahtīn	TW	summer
3.1.7	涼	lèuhng	Adj	cool
3.1.8	值得睇	jihkdāk tái	PH	worth-seeing

3.1.9	歷史	lihksí	N	history
3.1.10	建築	ginjūk	N	architecture
3.1.11	自然	jihyìhn	N	nature
3.1.12	風景	fūnggíng	N	scenary
3.1.13	南部	nàahm bouh	N	southern part
3.1.14	夠	gau	Adj	enough
3.1.15	辦簽證	baahn chīmjing	V	to apply for visa
3.1.16	麻煩	màhfàahn	Adj	troublesome
3.1.17	填表	tìhnbíu	V	to fill in form
3.1.18	影相	yíngséung	V	to take photograph
3.1.19	準備	jéunbeih	V	to prepare
3.1.20	證明	jingmìhng	V/N	to prove, proof
3.1.21	文件	màhngín	N	document
3.1.22	俾錢	béichín	V	to pay
3.1.23	問	mahn	V	to ask
3.1.24	睇到	táidóu	PH	saw, can be seen
3.1.25	方向	fōngheung	N	direction
3.1.26	行	hàahng	V	to walk
3.1.27	路口	louhháu	N	road junction
3.1.28	轉左	jyunjó	V	to turn left

3.2 Proper nouns

3.2.1	倫敦	Lèuhndēun	PW	London
3.2.2	海岸	hóingohn	PW	seashore
3.2.3	世界大樓	Saigaai daaihlàuh	Name	World Building
3.2.4	展覽中心	Jínláahm Jūngsām	N	exhibition centre

4. Notes on language structures
語言結構知識 yúhyìhn gitkau jīsīk

4.1 Structure notes

4.1.1 Verb-object (VO) structure

In Cantonese, some verbs do not need to take object while some verbs can take objects. The Verb-object compound is a verb compound composed by a verb and an object. The object attached is an obligatory component. If the object in VO is dropped, the meaning of the VO compound is incomplete or unclear.

4.1.2 Comparative constructions

"Adj-gwo" is used to compare two objects or two actions to show that one is more or less superior. The basic form of "Adj-gwo" is that superior noun placed before "Adj-gwo".

N1 Adj-gwo N2

Examples

Hēunggóng yihtgwo ngóhge gwokgā

Néihge sáudói lenggwo ngóhge.

Ngóh gōu gwo ngóh jèhjē (elder sister) hóu dō.

Manner of actions can also be compared using this structure.

N1 V-dāk-Adj-gwo N2

Examples

Kéuih hàahngdāk faai gwo ngóh.

Néih pàhngyáuh máaihyéh máaihdāk dō gwo ngóh.

Ngóh màhmā jyúfaahn jyúdāk hóusihk gwo chēutméngge jáudim (famous hotels).

4.1.3 "waahkjé" and "dihnghaih"

Both "waahkjé" and "dihnghaih" both mean "or". "waahkjé" is usually used in statements. "dihnghaih" is used in questions.

Examples

Gàmmáahn sihk Yahtbún choi waahkjé Hòhngwok choi (Korea food) dōu dāk.

Ngóh m̀geidāk néih pàhngyáuh géisìh làih Hēunggóng, gāmyaht dihnghaih tīngyaht a?

Nīgo touchāan (set meal) sung yámbán (drinks), néih jūngyi gafē dihnghaih náaihchàh a?

4.1.4   The use of "tùhng" and "yātchàih"

In Cantonese, "tùhng" is a co-verb meaning "and". It is a short form of "tùhngmàaih".

N tùhng N
V tùhng V
TW tùhng TW
Examples

Ngóh bàhbā tùhng màhmā hahgo yuht wúih làih taam ngóh.

Ngóh dākhàahn jūngyi yàuhséui tùhng dábō.

Gāmyaht tùhng tīngyaht ngóhdeih dōum̀dākhàahn. Hahgo láihbaai hóyíh gin néih.

"tùhng" and "tùhngmàaih" can be used to mean "together with". They can be used together with "yātchàih" meaning "together" to form a sentence pattern.

S1 tùhng S2 yātchàih V
Eamples

Ngóh tùhng néih yātchàih heui táihei lā.

Néih jīm̀jī kéuih kàhmyaht tùhng bīngo yātchàih sihkfaahn a?

Ngóh séung heui Hóiyèuhng gūngyún, néih hóm̀hóyíh tùhng ngóh yātchàih heui a?

The negative form of this structure is formed by putting "m̀" in front of "tùhng".

S1m̀tùhng S2 yātchàih V
Examples

Ngóh gāmyahtm̀dākhàahn, ngóh m̀tùhng néih yātchàih sihkfaahn la.

Kéuihm̀séung tùhng néih yātchàih heui tái nīchēut hei, ngóh tùhng néih heui.

Ngóh hahgo láihbaai yiu heui Méihgwok gūnggon. Ngóhm̀hóyíh tùhng néih yātchàih heui Yahtbún léuihhàhng.

Choice-type questions are formed by using "tùhngm̀tùhng…a?"
S1 tùhngm̀tùhng S2 yātchàih V a?
Examples

Ngóhdeih gāmmáahn heui kā lā ōu kē (karaoke), néih tùhngm̀tùhng ngóhdeih yātchàih heui a?

4.1.5 The use of "juhng" (also)

"juhng" means "also". "juhng" can be used with sentence-end particle, "tīm", to emphasize the meaning of "still.. more". It can also be used with "m̀jí" in "m̀jí… juhng" which has the same function as "not only…, but also" in English.

Examples

Juhng yáuh yātgo yàhn wúih làih, ngóhdeih dáng yāt dáng.

Ngóh m̀jí yáuh gòhgō jèhjē, juhng yáuh yāt go mùihmúi tùhng léuhng go dàihdái tīm.

Ngóh juhng tóuhngoh (hungry), ngóh juhng séung sihk dōdī tīm.

4.1.6 "daap" and "chóh" as a co-verb telling means of transportation

"chóh" literally means "to sit", as in "chíng chóh" (please sit). "chóh" can also be used together with means of transportation, e.g. "fóchē" (train), "bāsí" (bus), "dīksí" (taxi), "syùhn" (boat/ferry) &"fēigēi" (plane) to indicate the conveyance of coming or going to a place.

S daap/chóh … làih/heui/fāan PW

Examples

Hái Hēunggóng daap fēigēi heui Yahtbún yiu géinoih a?

Néih jīm̀jī daap fēigēi heui Tòihbāk (Taipei) yiu géidōchín a?

Gāmyaht dáfūng (typhoon), néih pàhngyáuh chóh fēigēi làih Hēunggóng, yáuh móuh mahntàih a?

4.1.7 Resultative verb "dóu"

A verb or an adjective can be affixed to an action verb to indicate that the verb has met its goal and the action has been completed successfully. "dóu" is one of the commonly used complements of result. In Cantonese, both action and result are necessary parts of the expression, therefore a result complement compound is treated as a verb, named Resultative verb, in a sentence. Sentence-end particle, "la", can be added at the end of the sentence to emphasize the change of status. "m̀" can be put between the verb and the result complement to show that the result cannot be achieved, as in "tái m̀dóu".

Examples

Ngóh kàhmyaht lódóu heui Méihgwok ge chīmjing (Visa) la.

Ngóh tēng m̀dóu, néih hóm̀hóyíh daaihsēng dī (louder) a?

Néih m̀daai ngáahngéng (not wear glasses), tái m̀táidóu a?

4.1.8 Asking and giving direction (Con't)

"hàahng", "jihkhàahng", "jyun…" and "dou" are verbs often used when giving directions.

Examples

Hái nīdouh jihkhàahng, néih wúih gindóu fóchē jaahm. Gindóu fóchē jaahm néih yiu jyun jó, jīhauh yātjihk hàahng. Hàahng sahp fānjūng jauh dou ngóh ūkkéi laak.

5 Notes on pragmatic knowledge

語用知識注解 yúhyuhng jīsīk jyugáai

5.1 How to find travel companion

5.1.1 Making decision

"yiu tái…" (depending on…) is used before the situation when making a decision.

Examples

Yātchàih heui BBQ hóu hóu, daahnhaih yiu tái tīnhei hóum̀hóu.

Ngóh pàhngyáuh hóu mòhng. Néih nīgo láihbaai séung gin kéuih, yiu tái kéuih dāk m̀dākhàahn.

Néih séung syúga (summer vacation) heui Yahtbún, yiu tái yáuh móuh gēipiu.

5.1.2 Introducing a different topic (interruping while others are speaking)

"haih la" can be used when you want to introduce a different topic in a conversation.

Examples

A: Syúga ngóhdeih yātchàih heui léuihhàhng, heui bīndouh hóu nē?

B: Heui Yahtbún hóu m̀hóu a? Ngóhdeih dōu meih heuigwo.

A: Yahtbún hóu! Ngóh hóu jūngyi Yahtbún, ngóh séung heui máaih hóudō yéh. Yaht bún gēipiu gwaiṁgwai nē?

B: Ngóh ṁjī a. Ngóhdeih hóyíh séuhngmóhng tái háh. Haih la. Néih gú Mary séungṁséung yātchàih heui nē?

A: Mary àh!? …

5.2 Related knowledge

5.2.1 Making a choice with "dihnghaih"

"dihnghaih" is used to provide options in a question or when making a selection after considering all the options. For the use of "dihnghaih", please refer to structure notes 4.1.3.

6 Contextualized speaking practice

情境說話練習 chìhnggíng syutwah lihnjaahp

6.1 Pronunciation Exercises and Situational Topics

A lady is asking the way to a hotel in Tsim Sha Tsui. She asks John and Mary how to get to the hotel. Please read aloud.

John 同 Mary 喺沙田飲茶，一個小姐問路。	John tùhng Mary hái Sātìhn yámchàh, yātgo síujé mahnlouh.
小姐：先生，小姐，請問（你哋）喺呢度 _____ 去半島酒店呀？	Síujé:Sīnsāang, síujé, chíngmahn (néihdeih) hái nīdouh _____ heui Bundóu Jáudim a?
John：喺呢度你 _____ 火車去九龍塘。喺九龍塘搭地鐵去尖沙咀。半島酒店喺尖沙咀。	John:Hái nīdouh néih _____ fóchē heui Gáulùhng Tòhng. Hái Gáulòhng Tòhng daap deihtit heui Jīmsājéui. Bundóu Jáudim hái Jīmsājéui.
小姐：而家 _____ 地鐵好多人…	Síujé:Yìhgā _____ deihtit hóu dō yàhn…

Mary：如果你唔想搭地鐵，你可以搭巴士 ＿＿＿＿＿ 小巴，但係（你）要等好耐。	Mary:Yùhgwó néihm̀séung daap deihtit, néih hóyíh daap bāsí ＿＿＿＿ síubā, daahnhaih(néih) yiu dáng hóunoih.
小姐：我唔可以遲到。點去最快呀？	Síujé:Ngóhm̀hóyíh chìhdou. Dím heui jeui faai a?
John：搭的士 ＿＿＿＿＿。你搭的士啦。	John:Daap dīksí ＿＿＿＿. Néih daap dīksí lā.
小姐：要幾多錢呀？	Síujé: Yiu géidō chín a?
John：＿＿＿＿＿ 一百二十蚊。	John: ＿＿＿＿ yātbaak yihsahp mān.
小姐：＿＿＿＿＿。	Síujé: ＿＿＿＿.
John & Mary：唔使唔該。	John & Mary:M̀sáim̀gōi.

6.2 Speech Topics

1. Néihge pàhngyáuh séung heui néih ngūkkéi taam néih, daahnhaih kéuihm̀jī néih ngūkkéi hái bīndouh. Chéng néih góng néihge deihjí béi kéuih tēng.

   你嘅朋友想去你屋企探你，但係佢唔知你屋企喺邊度。請你講你嘅地址俾佢聽。

   Your friend wants to visit you, but he/she does not know where do you live. Please tell him/her your address.

2. Néih haih yātgāan léuihhàhng séh ge beisyū, yìhgā yáuh yàhn dá dihnwá làih tàuhsou. Chéng néih góngháh kéuih tàuhsou dī mātyéh tùhng néih dím chyúhléih.

   你係一間旅行社嘅秘書，而家有人打電話嚟投訴。請你講吓佢投訴啲乜嘢同你點處理。

   You are the secretary of a travel agency. Now someone is phoning to complain. Please describe the complaint and how you handle it.

7. Listening and speaking

聽説練習 tingsyut lihnjaahp

7.1 On campus

安德：	聽講你爸爸喺台北做嘢，係唔係呀？	Ōndāk:	Tēnggóng néih bàhbā hái Tòihbāk jouhyéh, haih m̀haih a?
劉正風：	係呀，佢公司喺台北。我時時去探佢.	Làuh Jingfūng:	Haih a, kéuih gūngsī hái Tòihbāk. Ngóh sìhsìh heui taam kéuih.
安德：	嗽，你介紹幾個值得去嘅地方俾我啦。我打算去台北旅行。	Ōndāk:	Gám, néih gaaisiuh géigo jihkdāk heui ge deihfōng béi ngóh lā. Ngóh dásyun heui Tòihbāk léuihhàhng.
劉正風：	好呀，你想幾時去呀？	Làuh Jingfūng:	Hóu a, néih séung géisìh heui a?
安德：	六月或者十月，我仲未決定。	Ōndāk:	Luhkyuht waahkjé sahpyuht, ngóh juhng meih kyutdihng.
劉正風：	我覺得你十月去比較好。	Làuh Jingfūng:	Ngóh gokdāk néih sahpyuht heui béigaau hóu.
安德：	點解呢？	Ōndāk:	Dímgáai nē?
劉正風：	六月天氣唔好，又潮濕又熱，有時仲會落大雨，打風。	Làuh Jingfūng:	Luhkyuht tīnhei m̀hóu, yauh chìuhsāp yauh yiht, yáuhsìh juhng wúih lohk daaihyúh, dáfūng.
安德：	好，我就十月去啦。	Ōndāk:	Hóu, ngóh jauh sahpyuht heui lā.
劉正風：	係喇，十月我會喺台北，可以同你一齊玩。我姐姐同妹妹都可以做你嘅導遊。	Làuh Jingfūng:	Haih laak, sahpyuht ngóh wúih hái Tòihbāk, hóyíh tùhng néih yātchàih wáan. Ngóh jèhjē tùhng mùihmúi dōu hóyíh jouh néihge douhyàuh.
安德：	好呀！	Ōndāk:	Hóu a!

Lesson 9 Traveling in Hong Kong
暢遊香港

1. Contexts and linguistic functions
語境特徵與語言功能 *yúhgíng dahkjīng yúh yúhyìhn gūngnàhng*

Contexts (who, where, when) 語境特徵（人地時）	Linguistic functions 語言功能
Who: friends, new acquaintance **Where:** gathering with friend etc **When:** general	**Core functions:** Asking for help 求助
Language Scenarios: General situations, e.g. gathering with friends 一般情況，如朋友聚會	**Supplementary functions:** Asking for general information 獲取信息

Notes on pragmatic knowledge	Notes on language structures
I. What to say when seeking help 　1. Revisit various meaning of "dím" 　2. Asking for help: "dímsyun" II. Related knowledge 　1. The use of "yáuh yàhn"	- Directional complements - Comparative construction

2. Texts
課文 fomàhn

2.1 On school campus

安德：	正風，你好。歡迎你嚟我哋學校參觀。	**Ōndāk:**	Jingfūng, néih hóu. Fūnyìhng néih làih ngóhdeih hohkhaauh chāamgūn.
劉正風：	多謝你嚟接我。你哋學校離市區唔係幾遠。	**Làuh Jingfūng:**	Dōjeh néih làih jip ngóh. Néihdeih hohkhaauh lèih síhkēui m̀haih géi yúhn.
安德：	係呀，喺中環坐地鐵嚟，只係要四十五分鐘。	**Ōndāk:**	Haih a, hái Jūngwàahn chóh deihtit làih, jíhaih yiu seisahpńgh fānjūng.
劉正風：	你嘅宿舍喺邊度呀？	**Làuh Jingfūng:**	Néihge sūkséh hái bīndouh a?
安德：	喺山上便，行上去，會好攰，我哋坐車上去。	**Ōndāk:**	Hái sāan seuhngbihn, hàahng séuhngheui, wúih hóu guih, ngóhdeih chóhchē séuhngheui.
劉正風：	幾點有車呀？	**Làuh Jingfūng:**	Géidím yáuh chē a?
安德：	三點半有車，我地喺呢度等啦。	**Ōndāk:**	Sāamdím bun yáuh chē, ngóhdeih hái nīdouh dáng lā.
劉正風：	使唔使買飛呀？	**Làuh Jingfūng:**	Sáim̀sái máaih fēi a?
安德：	唔使。	**Ōndāk:**	M̀sái.
劉正風：	呢度嘅環境真係唔錯。哎呀！	**Làuh Jingfūng:**	Nīdouhge wàahngíng jānhaihm̀cho. Āiya!
安德：	乜嘢事呀？	**Ōndāk:**	Mātyéh sih a?

劉正風：	我嘅銀包唔見咗。點算呀？	**Làuh Jingfūng:**	Ngóhge ngàhnbāau m̀ginjó. Dímsyun a?
安德：	係唔係留咗喺火車上便呀？	**Ōndāk:**	Haihm̀haih làuhjó hái fóchē seuhngbihn a?
劉正風：	我都唔知道。	**Làuh Jingfūng:**	Ngóh dōu m̀jīdou.
安德：	我陪你去火車站問下啦。	**Ōndāk:**	Ngóh pùih néih heui fóchējaahm mahnháh lā.

2.2 In a shopping mall

安德：	我哋想去火車站接朋友先，之後去參觀博物館。	**Ōndāk:**	Ngóhdeih séung heui fóchē jaahm jip pàhngyáuh sīn, jīhauh heui chāamgūn bokmahtgún.
劉正風：	噉，你地坐的士去火車站啦。	**Làuh Jingfūng:**	Gám, néihdeih chóh dīksí heui fóchējaahm lā.
安德：	坐的士去，大概要幾多錢呀？	**Ōndāk:**	Chóh dīksí heui, daaihkoi yiu géidōchín a?
劉正風：	最多三十蚊。落車嗰陣時要攞收據。	**Làuh Jingfūng:**	Jeui dō sāamsahp mān. Lohkchē gójahnsìh yiu ló sāugeui.
安德：	收據係乜嘢呀？點解要攞收據呀？	**Ōndāk:**	Sāugeui haih mātyéh a? Dímgáai yiu ló sāugeui a?
劉正風：	收據上便有的士嘅車牌號碼，如果你留咗嘢喺車上便…	**Làuh Jingfūng:**	Sāugeui seuhngbihn yáuh dīksí ge chēpàaih houhmáh, yùhgwó néih làuhjó yéh hái chēseuhngbihn…
安德：	明白，有呢個號碼，我哋就可以搵到呢架車。	**Ōndāk:**	Mìhngbaahk, yáuh nīgo houhmáh, ngóhdeih jauh hóyíh wándóu nīga chē.

| 劉正風： | 係喇，噉就可以幫你搵返啲嘢。 | **Làuh Jingfūng:** | Haih la, gám jauh hóyíh bōng néih wánfāan dīyéh. |

2.3 At the airport

安德：	對唔住，麻煩你幫一幫我。	**Ōndāk:**	Deuimjyuh, màhfàahn néih bōng yāt bōng ngóh.
職員：	有乜嘢事呀？	**Jīkyùhn:**	Yáuh mātyéh sih a?
安德：	我坐嘅火車遲咗，而家趕唔到呢班飛機。我應該點做呀？	**Ōndāk:**	Ngóh chóhge fóchē chìhjó, yìhgā gónṁdóu nībāan fēigēi. Ngóh yīnggōi dím jouh a?
職員：	等我睇一睇你嘅機票。呢種機票唔可以改期。	**Jīkyùhn:**	Dáng ngóh tái yāt tái néihge gēipiu. Nījúng gēipiu ṁhóyíh góikèih.
安德：	你嘅意思係我唔可以改坐下一班機？	**Ōndāk:**	Néihge yisī haih ngóh ṁhóyíh gói chóh hah yāt bāan gēi?
職員：	係呀，你要另外買一張機票。	**Jīkyùhn:**	Haih a, néih yiu lihngngoih máaih yātjēung gēipiu.
安德：	噉，我呢張機票可唔可以退錢呀？	**Ōndāk:**	Gám, ngóh nījēung gēipiu hóṁhóyíh teuichín a?
職員：	噉，我就唔清楚喇。你要聯絡客戶服務中心。	**Jīkyùhn:**	Gám, ngóh jauh ṁchīngchó la. Néih yiu lyùhnlok haakwuh fuhkmouh jūngsām.
安德：	好啦。噉，下班機有冇位呀？	**Ōndāk:**	Hóu lā. Gám, hahbāan gēi yáuhmóuh wái a?
職員：	仲有位。	**Jīkyùhn:**	Juhngyáuh wái.

3. Vocabulary in use

活用詞彙 wuhtyuhng chìh wuih

3.1 Common vocabulary

Number	Word	Yale Romanization	POS	English
3.1.1	參觀	chāamgūn	V	to visit a place
3.1.2	地鐵	deihtit	N	MTR, subway
3.1.3	只係	jíhaih	Adv	only
3.1.4	分鐘	fānjūng	N	minute
3.1.5	坐車	chóh chē	V	to ride in a car
3.1.6	唔使	m̀sái	PH	no need
3.1.7	環境	wàahngíng	N	environment
3.1.8	真係	jānhaih	Adv	really
3.1.9	唔錯	m̀cho	PH	not bad
3.1.10	銀包	ngàhnbāau	N	purse
3.1.11	唔見咗	m̀ginjó	PH	be missing; to be lost
3.1.12	點算	dímsyun	QW	what can be done
3.1.13	留咗喺火車上便	làuhjó hái fóchē seuhngbihn	PH	left in the train
3.1.14	陪	pùih	V	to accompany
3.1.15	的士	dīksí	N	taxi
3.1.16	最多	jeui dō	PH	the most
3.1.17	落車	lohkchē	V	to take off car
3.1.18	攞	ló	V	to take, to bring
3.1.19	收據	sāugeui	N	receipt
3.1.20	車牌	chē pàaih	N	car licence, car number plate; driving licence

3.1.21	明白	mìhngbaahk	V	to understand
3.1.22	搵返	wánfāan	PH	found, to be found
3.1.23	遲咗	chìhjó	PH	to be late
3.1.24	趕唔到	gón m̀dóu	PH	cannot catch (vehicle)
3.1.25	呢班飛機	nībāan fēigēi	PH	this airplane
3.1.26	應該	yīnggōi	AV	should
3.1.27	點做	dímjouh	QW	what to do
3.1.28	機票	gēipiu	N	air ticket
3.1.29	改	gói	V	to change, to correct
3.1.30	另外	lihngngoih	Adv	another, other
3.1.31	退錢	teuichín	V	to refund
3.1.32	唔清楚	m̀chīngchó	PH	not clear
3.1.33	聯絡	lyùhnlok	V	to be in touch (with people)

3.2 Proper nouns

3.2.1	劉正風	Làuh Jing Fūng	Name	Lau Jing Fung
3.2.2	市區	síhkēui	PW	city area
3.2.3	中環	Jūngwàahn	PW	Central
3.2.4	客戶服務中心	haakwuh fuhkmouh jūngsām	N	customer service centre

4. Notes on Language structures

語言結構知識 *yúhyìhn gitkau jīsīk*

4.1 Structure notes

4.1.1 Directional complements

The attachement of "làih" and "heui" to directional verbs, such as "séung" (up), "lohk" (down), "fāan" (return) &"gwo" (go pass), etc; is a distinctive feature of Cantonese. These complements are used to indicate whether an action "comes" ("làih") towards the speaker or "goes" ("heui") away from the speaker.

Séuhng/lohk

Fāan làih/heui

gwo

Examples

Néih hóm̀hóyíh séuhngheui làuhseuhng (upstairs) bōng ngóh ló nīdī yéh béi ngóh bàhbā a?

Sānnìhn gójahnsìh, hái Gwóngjāu fóchē jaahm fāanheui ūkkéi ge yàhn hóu dō.

M̀goi néih gwolàih béi ngóh táiháh néih séjó dī mātyéh.

A compound directional complement can be formed by adding "hàahng" (to walk), "jáu" (to run), "chóh bāsí" (to tke a bus).

Examples

Ngóh hàahng lohkheui ngàhnhòhng lóchín (get money).

Ngóhge pàhngyáuh chóh fēigēi fāan heui kéuihge gwokgā.

M̀hóu jáu lohkheui a! Hóu ngàihhím (dangerous) ga!

4.1.2 Comparative construction (Con't)

The use of "dī" after adjectives is another way to show comparative.

Examples

Kéuih géi gōu, kéuih bàhbā gōudī.

Kàhmyaht yiht gwo gāmyaht, daahnhaih hah sīngkèih yihtdī.

Heui Yahtbún hóu gwai, heui Méihgwok gwaidī.

5. Notes on pragmatic knowledge

語用知識注解 yúhyuhng jīsīk jyugáai

5.1 What to say when seeking help

5.1.1 Revisit various meanings of "dím"

"dím" can be used as greeting in "néih dím a?", "dím a?", "jeuigahn dím a?" (how are you recently) in casual settings when you come across a friend who has not met after a while.

Examples

Tēnggóng (I heard that) néih behngjó, néih dím a?

5.1.2 Asking for help "dím syun"

"dím syun a?" is used when you need advice on what to do.

Examples

Heui sihkfaahn, màaihdāan gójahnsìh faatgok (discover) móuh chín, dím syun nē?

Tīngyaht háausíh, juhng meih duhksyū (study), dím syun a?

Yìhgā taai yeh (too late at night), móuh chē fāan ūkkéi, dím syun a?

5.2 Related knowledge

5.2.1 The use of "yáuh yàhn"

"yáuh yàhn" literally means "there are people". It can be used to indicate "someone…", as in "yáuh yàhn wah néih hóu leng" (someone said you are pretty) and "yáuh yàhn wán néih" (someone looks for you).

6. Contextualized speaking practice

情境説話練習 chìhnggíng syutwah lihnjaahp

6.1 Pronunciation Exercises and Situational Topics

Lisa's parents are visiting Hong Kong. Lisa and A Mei are talking about some good places to show Lisa's parents. Please read aloud.

Laihsā ge fuhmóuh jauhlàih hái Méihgwok chóh fēigēi làih Hēunggóng wáan la, A-Mēi mahn Laihsā:
麗莎嘅父母就嚟喺美國坐飛機嚟香港玩嘑，亞美問麗莎：

亞美：	你打算帶佢哋去邊度玩呀？	**A Mēi:**	Néih dásyun daai kéuihdeih heui bīndouh wáan a?
麗莎：	香港最靓嘅就係山頂。我會同父母喺中文大學坐火車去九龍塘，之後轉地鐵到尖沙咀，喺尖沙咀碼頭坐船去中環，之後行去纜車站，喺嗰度坐纜車去山頂。	**Laihsā:**	Hēunggóng jeui lengge jauhhaih Sāandéng. Ngóh wúih tùhng fuhmóuh hái Jūngmàhn Daaihhohk chóh fóchē heui Gáulùhngtòhng, jīhauh jyun deihtit dou Jīmsājéui, hái Jīmsājéui máhtàuh chóh syùhn heui Jūngwàahn, jīhauh hàahngheui LaahmchēJaahm, hái gódouh chóh laahmchē heui Sāandéng.
亞美：	你想日頭去定夜晚去山頂呀？	**A Mēi:**	Néih séung yahttáu heui dihng yehmáahn heui Sāandéng a?
麗莎：	香港嘅夜景咁出名，我哋梗係夜晚去啦！	**Laihsā:**	Hēunggóng ge yehgíng gam chēutméng, ngóhdeih gánghaih yehmáahn heui lā!
亞美：	如果想睇夜景，你都可以去尖沙咀海邊行吓，嗰度唔止平時靓，每年聖誕節，嗰度嘅燈飾都好靓。所以好多人會同家人、朋友去嗰度睇燈飾，個個人都好開心。你仲會同父母去邊度玩呀？	**A Mēi:**	Yùhgwó séung tái yehgíng, néih dōu hóyíh heui Jīmsājéui hóibīn hàahnghháh, gódouhm̀jí pìhngsìh leng, múihnìhn Singdaanjit, gódouh ge dāngsīk dōu hóu leng. Sóyíhhóudō yàhn wúih tùhng gāyàhn, pàhngyáuh heui gódouh tái dāngsīk, gogo yàhn dōuhóu hōisām. Néih juhngwúih tùhng fuhmóuh heui bīndouh wáan a?
麗莎：	我媽媽好鍾意買嘢，我梗係會帶佢去赤柱、銅鑼灣同女人街買嘢啦。如果爸爸唔癐，我都想同佢去吓廟街。	**Laihsā:**	Ngóh màhmā hóu jūngyi máaihyéh, ngóh gánghaih wúih daai kéuih heui Chekchyúh, Tùhnglòhwāahn tùhng Néuihyán Gāai máaihháh yéh lā. Yùhgwó bàhbām̀guih, ngóh dōu séung tùhng kéuih heuiháhMíu Gāai.
亞美：	點解要同爸爸去廟街呢？	**A Mēi:**	Dímgáai yiu tùhng bàhbā heui Míu Gāai nē?

麗莎：	哦！因為有啲書話廟街係男人街，好多男人都會去嗰度行吓。	**Laihsā:**	Óh! Yānwaih yáuh dī syū wah Míu Gāai haih nàahmyán gāai, hóudō nàahmyán dōu wúih heui gódouh hàahngháh.
亞美：	係咩！香港嘅海鮮都好出名，你會帶佢哋去食嗎？	**A Mēi:**	Haih mē! Hēunggóng ge hóisīn dōu hóu chēutméng, néih wúihdaai kéuihdeih heui sihk ma?
麗莎：	我想帶佢哋喺彩虹地鐵站坐小巴去西貢食海鮮。	**Laihsā:**	Ngóh séung daai kéuihdeih hái Chói Hùhng deihtitjaahm chóh síubā heui Sāigung sihk hóisīn.
亞美：	你都可以喺中環坐船去南丫島食海鮮。	**A Mēi:**	Néih dōu hóyíh hái Jūngwàahn chóh syùhn heui Nàahm Ā Dóu sihk hóisīn.
麗莎：	冇錯。不過去南丫島玩，我怕唔夠時間，因為佢哋都想去吓澳門。	**Laihsā:**	Móuhcho, bātgwo heui Nàahm Ā Dóu wáan, ngóh paṁgau sìhgaan, yānwaih kéuihdeih dōu séung heuiháh Ngoumún.
亞美：	澳門嘅手信好出名。噉，你去澳門嗰陣時，要買啲手信噃！	**A Mēi:**	Ngoumún ge sáuseun hóu chēutméng. Gám, Néih heui Ngoumún gójahnsìh, yiu máaihdī sáuseun bo!

6.2 Speech Topics

1. Néihge yātgo Méihgwok pàhngyáuh làih Hēunggóng taam néih, néih wúih daai kéuih heui bīndouh wáan a? Néih wúih dím tùhng kéuih heui nē?

   你嘅一個美國朋友嚟香港探你，你會帶佢去邊度玩呀？你會點同佢去呢？

   Your American friend will come to Hong Kong to visit you. Where will you bring him/her to tour? How will you go with him/her?

2. Hái Hēunggóng néih jeui jūngyi chóh mātyéh chē a? Chéng góng béi ngóhdeihtēng néih dímgáai gam jūngyi chóh nī júng chē nē? Néih wúih chóh nī júng chē heui bīndouh wáan nē?

   喺香港你最鍾意坐乜嘢車呀？請講俾我哋聽你點解咁鍾意坐呢種車呢？你會坐呢種車去邊度玩呢？

   What kind of transportation in Hong Kong do you like the most? Please tell us why you like it so much, and where you like to go with this transportation.

7. Listening and speaking

聽説練習 tingsyut lihnjaahp

7.1 In the dormitory

安德：	阿王，我地想去九寨溝旅行，你覺得點樣去比較好呀？	**Ōndāk:**	A Wóng, ngóhdeih séung heui Gáujaaihkāu léuihhàhng, néih gokdāk dímyéung heui béigaau hóu a?
阿王：	要睇你地打算幾時去。	**A Wóng:**	Yiu tái néihdeih dásyun géisìh heui.
安德：	我地想農曆新年去。	**Ōndāk:**	Ngóhdeih séung nùhnglihk sānnìhn heui.
阿王：	春季同秋季遊客特別多，跟旅行團去比較方便。	**A Wóng:**	Chēun gwai tùhng chāugwai yàuhhaak dahkbiht dō, gān léuihhàhng tyùhn heui béigaau fōngbihn.
安德：	我地比較鍾意自己去。	**Ōndāk:**	Ngóhdeih béigaau jūngyi jihgéi heui.
阿王：	噉，就要早啲訂飛同酒店喇。	**A Wóng:**	Gám, jauh yiu jóudī dehng fēi tùhng jáudim la.
安德：	我地搵緊，不過仲未搵到平嘅。	**Ōndāk:**	Ngóhdeih wángán, bātgwo juhngmeih wándóu pèhngge.
阿王：	我覺得你地仲係參加旅行團啦。噉樣會平啲。	**A Wóng:**	Ngóh gokdāk néihdeih juhnghaih chāamgā léuihhàhng tyùhn lā. Gámyéung wúih pèhngdī.

7.2 In the dormitory

子安：	請問，安德喺唔喺度呀？	**Jíon:**	Chíngmahn, Ōndāk hái m̀hái douh a?
阿王：	安德，有人搵你。	**A Wóng:**	Ōndāk, yáuh yàhn wán néih.
安德：	子安，你好。請坐。點呀？就快放假喇。	**Ōndāk:**	Jíon, néih hóu. Chíng chóh. Dim a? Jauh faai fongga la.

子安：	係呀，放假嗰陣時，我打算去泰國玩。	**Jíōn:**	Haih a, fongga gójahnsìh, ngóh dásyun heui Taaigwok wáan.
安德：	好呀，我上個月去過。嗰度有好多小島，風景好靚，你可以喺嗰度玩下、休息下。	**Ōndāk:**	Hóu a, ngóh seuhnggo yuht heuigwo. Gódouh yáuh hóudō síudóu, fūnggíng hóu leng, néih hóyíh hái gódouh wáanháh, yāusīkháh.
子安：	噉就好喇，我就係想輕鬆下。	**Jíōn:**	Gám jauh hóu la, ngóh jauh haih séung hīngsūngháh.

Lesson 10 Saying goodbye and farewell
講聲再見

1. Contexts and linguistic functions
語境特徵與語言功能 *yúhgíng dahkjīng yúh yúhyìhn gūngnàhng*

Contexts (who, where, when) 語境特徵（人地時）	Linguistic functions 語言功能
Who: friends **Where:** school, casual gathering, office, etc **When:** general	**Core functions:** Expressing gratitude (informal) 致謝（非正式）
Language Scenarios: General situations, e.g. school campus, office 一般情況，如校園、公司	**Supplementary functions:** Describing 描述

Notes on pragmatic knowledge	Notes on language structures
I. How to express gratutide and saying "goodbye" (semi-formal) 　1. Expressing congratulations 　2. Expressing good wishes II. Related Knowledge 　1. Saying farewell	- If⋯, then⋯: "Yùhgwó⋯jauh⋯" - The use of "tùhng" meaning "for" - The use of "-yùhn" to indicate finished action - More use of "jauh" as an adverb - Becoming more and more: "yuht làih yuht…", "yuht V yuht…"

2. Texts

課文 fomàhn

2.1 In the classroom

德華：	呢次旅行點呀？	**Dākwàh:**	Nīchi léuihhàhng dím a?
安德：	非常好。桂林山水好特別，同我見過嘅好唔同。	**Ōndāk:**	Fēisèuhng hóu. Gwailàhm sāanséui hóu dahkbiht, tùhng ngóh gingwo ge hóuṁtùhng.
德華：	你地有冇去陽朔呀？	**Dākwàh:**	Néihdeih yáuhmóuh heui Yèuhngsok a?
安德：	去咗，我地喺桂林坐船去。	**Ōndāk:**	Heuijó, ngóhdeih hái Gwailàhm chóh syùhn heui.
德華：	聽講嗰度風景靚過桂林。你覺得係唔係呀？	**Dākwàh:**	Tēnggóng gódouh fūnggíng lenggwo Gwailàhm. Néih gokdāk haihṁhaih a?
安德：	我覺得兩個地方嘅風景差唔多，不過陽朔靜啲，桂林嘅遊客太多，有啲嘈。	**Ōndāk:**	Ngóh gokdāk léuhnggo deihfōngge fūnggíng chāṁdō, bātgwo Yèuhngsok jihngdī, Gwailàhm ge yàuhhaak taai dō, yáuhdī chòuh.
德華：	嗰度地方好大，使唔使行好耐呀？攰唔攰呀？	**Dākwàh:**	Gódouh deihfōng hóudaaih, sái ṁsái hàahng hóunoih a? Guih ṁguih a?
安德：	我地踩單車，一邊踩單車一邊睇風景，又輕鬆又好玩。	**Ōndāk:**	Ngóhdeih cháai dāanchē, yātbīn cháai dāanchē yātbīn tái fūnggíng, yauh hīngsūng yauh hóuwáan.
德華：	踩單車，對我嚟講太難喇。我踩得唔好。	**Dākwàh:**	Cháai dāanchē, deui ngóh láih góng taai nàahn la. Ngóh cháaidāk ṁhóu.
安德：	喺嗰度，路上便車唔多，慢慢踩就得。	**Ōndāk:**	Hái gódouh, louh seuhngbihn chēṁdō, maahnmáan cháai jauh dāk.

德華：	除咗睇風景，你地喺嗰度，仲做咗啲乜嘢呀？	**Dākwàh:**	Chèuihjó tái fūnggíng, néihdeih hái gódouh, juhng jouhjó dī mātyéh a?
安德：	我地喺嗰度仲睇咗一個歌舞表演。	**Ōndāk:**	Ngóhdeih hái gódouh juhng táijó yātgo gōmóuh bíuyín.
德華：	值唔值得睇呀？	**Dākwàh:**	Jihk m̀jihkdāk tái a?
安德：	值得呀，我從來都冇睇過嗰樣嘅歌舞表演。	**Ōndāk:**	Jihkdāk a, ngóh chùhnglòih dōu móuh táigwo gám yéung ge gōmóuh bíuyín.
德華：	如果有時間，我都想去。	**Dākwàh:**	Yùhgwó yáuh sìhgaan, ngóh dōu séung heui.
安德：	如果你冇去過，就一定要去一次。	**Ōndāk:**	Yùhgwó néih móuh heuigwo, jauh yātdihng yiu heui yātchi.

2.2 On school campus

子安：	安德，時間過得好快，你下星期就要返德國喇。	**Jíōn:**	Ōndāk, sìhgaan gwodāk hóufaai, néih hahsīngkèih jauh yiu fāan Dākgwok la.
安德：	係呀，時間過得太快喇。	**Ōndāk:**	Haih a, sìhgaan gwodāk taai faai la.
子安：	我記得你嚟嗰陣時唔係幾鍾意香港。	**Jíōn:**	Ngóh geidāk néih làih gójahnsìh m̀haih géi jūngyi Hēunggóng.
安德：	係呀，我六月嚟，嗰陣時天氣又熱又濕，真係唔習慣。	**Ōndāk:**	Haih a, ngóh luhkyuht làih, gójahnsìh tīnhei yauh yiht yauh sāp, jānhaih m̀jaahpgwaan.
子安：	而家習慣未呀？	**Jíōn:**	Yìhgā jaahpgwaan meih a?
安德：	我而家都仲未習慣香港嘅夏天，不過我越嚟越鍾意香港。	**Ōndāk:**	Ngóh yìhgā dōu juhng meih jaahpgwaan Hēunggóngge hahtīn, bātgwo ngóh yuhtláih yuht jūngyi Hēunggóng,
子安：	你鍾意香港嘅邊方面呀？	**Jíōn:**	Néih jūngyi Hēunggóngge bīn fōngmihn a?

安德：	我鍾意香港，交通方便，好熱鬧，喺外邊食飯，選擇好多，唔係好貴。	Ōndāk:	Ngóh jūngyi Hēunggóng, gāautūng fōngbihn, hóu yihtnaauh, hái ngoihbihn sihkfaahn, syúnjaahk hóu dō, m̀haih hóu gwai.
子安：	噉，你想唔想喺香港搵嘢做呀？	Jíōn:	Gám, néih séung m̀séung hái Hēunggóng wán yéh jouh a?
安德：	如果有機會，我會試下。	Ōndāk:	Yùhgwó yáuh gēiwuih, ngóh wúih siháh.

2.3 In the farewell party

安德：	小文，多謝你嚟參加呢個歡送會。	Ōndāk:	Síumàhn, dōjeh néih làih chāamgā nīgo fūnsung wúi.
小文：	我都好開心見到你。聽講你好快就要返德國喇。	Síumàhn:	Ngóh dōu hóu hōisām gindóu néih. Tēnggóng néih hóu faai jauh yiu fāan Dākgwok la.
安德：	係呀，我下個月開始做嘢喇。	Ōndāk:	Haih a, ngóh hahgo yuht hōichí jouhyéh la.
小文：	嘩，已經搵到嘢做喇，恭喜你。係唔係返德國工作呀？	Síumàhn:	Wa, yíhgīng wándóu yéh jouh la, gūnghéi néih. Haih m̀haih fāan Dākgwok gūngjok a?
安德：	唔係呀，係喺美國紐約。你呢？畢業之後，有乜嘢打算呀？	Ōndāk:	M̀haih a, haih hái Méihgwok Náuyeuk. Néih nē? Bātyihp jīhauh, yáuh mātyéh dásyun a?
小文：	我搵緊嘢做，希望搵到合適嘅工作。	Síumàhn:	Ngóh wángán yéh jouh, hēimohng wándóu hahpsīkge gūngjok.
安德：	祝你成功。	Ōndāk:	Jūk néih sìhnggūng.
小文：	多謝你，我都祝你工作順利。	Síumàhn:	Dōjeh néih, ngóh dōu jūk néih gūngjok seuhnleih.

3. Vocabulary in use

活用詞彙 wuhtyuhng chìhwuih

3.1 Common vocabulary

Number	Word	Yale Romanization	POS	English
3.1.1	旅行	léuihhàhng	V/N	travel
3.1.2	……點呀？	…dím a?	PH	how is… ?
3.1.3	特別	dahkbiht	Adj	special
3.1.4	唔同	m̀tùhng	Adj	different
3.1.5	坐船	chóh syùhn	V	to take a ferry/boat
3.1.6	覺得	gokdāk	V	to feel
3.1.7	差唔多	chāﾑdō	Adj	almost the same, similar
3.1.8	靜啲	jihngdī	PH	quieter
3.1.9	遊客	yàuhhaak	N	tourist
3.1.10	有啲	yáuhdī	Adv	a little bit
3.1.11	嘈	chòuh	Adj	noisy
3.1.12	好耐	hóu noih	Adj	long time
3.1.13	癐	guih	Adj	tired
3.1.14	踩單車	cháai dāanchē	V	to ride on bicycle
3.1.15	輕鬆	hīngsūng	Adj	relaxed
3.1.16	好玩	hóu wáan	Adj	fun
3.1.17	對我嚟講太難	deui ngóh láih góng taai nàahn	PH	too difficult for me
3.1.18	路上便	louh seuhngbihn	PH	on the way; on the road
3.1.19	慢慢	maahnmáan	Adv	slowly; gradually
3.1.20	歌舞表演	gōmóuh bíuyín	N	singing and dancing show
3.1.21	噉樣	gám yéung	PH	in this way

3.1.22	如果	yùhgwó	Adv	if
3.1.23	一定	yātdihng	Adv	definitely
3.1.24	濕	sāp	Adj	wet; humid
3.1.25	習慣	jaahpgwaan	V/N	be used to; habit
3.1.26	邊方面？	bīn fōngmihn?	PH	which aspect?
3.1.27	交通	gāautūng	N	transportation
3.1.28	方便	fōngbihn	Adj	convenient
3.1.29	熱鬧	yihtnaauh	Adj	bustling
3.1.30	選擇	syúnjaahk	V/N	to choose, choice
3.1.31	搵嘢做	wán yéh jouh	PH	find job (lit. find things to do)
3.1.32	參加	chāamgā	V	to participate in
3.1.33	開始	hōichí	V	to start
3.1.34	做嘢	jouhyéh	V	to work (lit. to do things)
3.1.35	恭喜	gūnghéi	V	congratulate
3.1.36	工作	gūngjok	N	work
3.1.37	合適	hahpsīk	Adj	suitable
3.1.38	祝你成功	jūk néih sìhnggūng	PH	wish you success
3.1.39	工作順利	gūngjok seuhnleih	PH	best wishes in work

3.2 Proper nouns

3.2.1	桂林	Gwailàhm	PW	Guilin
3.2.2	陽朔	Yèuhngsok	PW	Yangshuo
3.2.3	紐約	Náuyeuk	PW	New York

4. Notes on language structures
語言結構知識 yúhyìhn gitkau jīsīk

4.1 Structure notes

4.1.1   If···, then···: "Yùhgwó···jauh···"

In Cantonese, "yùhgwó" means "if" and it forms a conditional sentence together with "jauh" (then). In the conditional sentence, the condition must appear in the Yùhgwó-clause before "jauh". The subject of the jauh-clause should always come before "jauh".

Yùhgwó…, (S) jauh…
In Cantonese conditional sentences, "yùhgwó" can be omitted.
(Yùhgwó)…, (S) jauh…

Example
Yùhgwó néih yáuh sìhgaan, néih jauh dá dihnwá béi ngóh lā.
Néih jyúfaahn, ngóh jauh yātdihng làih.
M̀lohkyúh, jauh heui BBQ.

4.1.2   The use of "tùhng" meaning "for"

In Cantonese, co-verb, "tùhng" can be used to mean "for". If it means "for" it cannot be replaced by "tùhngmàaih" and cannot be used with "yātchàih".

N1 tùhng N2 V
Examples
M̀gōi néih tùhng ngóh ló nīdī yéh béi kéuih, dāk m̀dāk a?
Ngóh gāmyaht behngjó, néih tùhng ngóh jyúfaahn dākm̀dāk a?
Ngóhm̀hóyíh tùhng néih jouh nīdī yéh.

4.1.3   The use of "-yùhn" to indicate finished action

In Cantonese, "-yùhn" is a verb suffix used to indicate a finished action. It is especially used to emphasize the action in progress is finished. "meih" is used as negation and it comes before the verb.

S V-yùhn O

S meih V-yùhn O

Examples

Ngóhdeih sihkyùhn faahn jouh mātyéh a?

Ṁgōi néih jouhyùhn jīhauh dá dihnwá béi ngóh.

Ngóh meih jouhyùhn, ṁhóyíh sihkfaahn.

The choice-type questions of "-yùhn" construction is formed by putting "meih" after "V-yùhn O", the choice is between "V-yùhn O" (V-finished) and "meih" (not yet).

S V-yùhn O meih a?

Examples

Néih duhkyùhn syū meih a?

Néihdeih sihkyùhn faahn meih a? Sihkyùhn ngóhdeih heui kā lā ōu kēi la.

Ngóh dángjó hóu noih la, néih jouhyùhn meih a?

4.1.4   More use of "jauh" as an adverb

"jauhlàih" in Cantonese means "soon". "jauh", here, is the short form of "jauhlàih". It must be placed after the subject and before the verb. It can go with a sentence-end particle, "la", to indicate a change of status.

"jauh…la" is used to indicate that an action or situation will occur in the immediate future. "hóu faai" (very soon) can also be used together.

S jauh/jauhlàih… (la)

Examples

Ṁsái gāp (hurry), jauhlàih dāk la.

Jauhlàih móuh chín la, dím syun a?

Faaidī jouh lā, jauhlàih gaujūng (time's up) la.

4.1.5   Comparative constructions (con't)

"…tùhng… yātyeuhng" is used to show two objects or two actions are in the same state. The negative "ṁ" is placed before "yātyeuhng" to mean "not the same". "…tùhng… chāṁdō" is used to mean "… and … are almost the same".

Examples

Ngóh tùhng néih yātyeuhng gam leng.

Gāmyaht tùhng kàhmyaht chāṁdō yātyeuhng gam yiht.

Hēunggóng tùhng Méihgwok ṁyātyeuhng, Hēunggóngge ūk (apartment/house) hóu sai.

"…móuh…gam Adj" is used to compare two objects or two actions. It is to say the former does not reach the degree of the latter.

Examples

Ngóh móuh néih gam lēk (smart).

Kéuih jāchē móuh ngóh jāchē gam ōnchyùhn (safe).

Ngóh màhmā jyúfaahn móuh ngóh bàhbā jyú dāk gam hóusihk.

4.1.6 Becoming more and more: "yuht làih yuht…" , "yuht V yuht…"
"yuht làih yuht…" is used before adjectives or modal verbs to describe the quality or the state of something is increasing. Adverbs, such as "hóu", "géi", "ṁhaih géi" cannot be used in "yuht làih yuht…" construction.

S yuht làih yuht Adj

Examples

Wa! Néih yuht làih yuht leng!

Hēunggóngge tīnhei yuht làih yuht yiht.

Néih yuht làih yuht fèih (fat),ṁhóu sihk taai dō la!

"yuht V yuht…" shows that the more the action (V) is carried out, the state of something is increasing. Same as "yuht làih yuht…" construction, adverbs, such as "hóu", "géi", "mhaih géi" cannot be used with the adjective.

S yuht V yuht Adj

Examples

Kéuih yuht góng yuht faai, ngóh jānhaih tēng ṁdóu kéuih góng mātyéh.

Nćih yuht góng, ngóh yuht ṁmìhngbaahk.

Gwóngdūng wá yuht hohk yuht nàahn. Néih hóṁhóyíh bōngháh ngóh a?

5. Notes on pragmatic knowledge

語用知識注解 *yúhyuhng jīsīk jyugáai*

5.1 How to express gratutide and saying "goodbye" (semi-formal)

5.1.1 Expressing congratulations

"gūnghéi, gūnghéi" is used for congratulating in various happy occasions both in formal and casual settings, such as in wedding ceremony, child birth and promotion, etc.

5.1.2 Expressing good wishes

"jūk néih" is used before the wish to express good wishes to the person, sometimes with the implication of congratulating.

Examples

Jūk néih sāangyaht faailohk! (Wish you happy birthday!)

Jūk néih sāntái gihnhōng! (Wish you good health!)

Jūk néih sìhnggūng (Wish you success!)

5.2 Related knowledge

5.2.1 Saying farewell

"joigin" is a "goodbye" used in everyday situations. "jūk néih yātlouh seuhnfūng" (Bon voyage) and "jūk néih sihsih seuhnleih" (wish everything goes smoothly) can be used to someone who is leaving for good.

6. Contextualized speaking practice

情境說話練習 *chìhnggíng syutwah lihnjaahp*

6.1 Pronunciation Exercises and Situational Topics

Andrew is leaving Hong Kong. Aaron is helping him to pack and depart. Please read aloud.

阿王：	安德，執好行李未呀？	**A Wóng:**	Ōndāk, jāphóu hàhngléih meih a?
安德：	差唔多喇。	**Ōndāk:**	Chāṁdō la.
阿王：	你有好多嘢，一個人可以帶咁多行李咩？	**A Wóng:**	Néih yáuh hóu dō yéh, yātgo yàhn hóyíh daai gam dō hàhngléih mē?
安德：	我唔打算自己帶，我要寄返去。	**Ōndāk:**	Ngóhṁdásyun jihgéi daai, ngóh yiu gei fāanheui.
阿王：	噉，我幫你叫的士，送你去郵局啦。	**A Wóng:**	Gám, ngóh bōng néih giu dīksí, sung néih heui yàuhgúk lā.
安德：	好呀，麻煩你喇。	**Ōndāk:**	Hóu a, màhfàahn néih la.
阿王：	唔使客氣。	**A Wóng:**	Ṁsái haakhei.
安德：	係喇，我有一個煲，仲有啲碟同碗，你要唔要呀？	**Ōndāk:**	Haih la, ngóh yáuh yātgo bōu, juhng yáuh dī díp tùhng wún, néih yiuṁyiu a?
阿王：	好呀，有幾個新同學，佢地一定需要呢啲嘢。	**A Wóng:**	Hóu a, yáuh géigo sān tùhnghohk, kéuihdeih yātdihng sēuiyiu nīdī yéh.
安德：	噉就好喇。	**Ōndāk:**	Gám jauh hóu la.

6.2 Speech Topics

1. Chéng néih gaaisiuhháh néihge gwokgā yáuhdī mātyéh gányiu ge jit yaht. Néih jeui jūngyi bīndī jit yaht nē? Dímgáai a?

   請你介紹吓你嘅國家有啲乜嘢緊要嘅節日。你最鍾意邊啲節日呢？點解呀？

   Please tell us the major festivals in your country. Which one do you like most? And why?

2. Néih yiu fāanheui jihgéi ge gwokgā, tùhnghohk hōi yātgo fūnsung wúi fūnsung néih. Néih hái fūnsung wúi seuhngbihn dōjeh néih ge lóuhsī, tùhnghohk tùhng pàhngyáuh.

   你要返去自己嘅國家，同學開一個歡送會歡送你。你喺歡送會上便多謝你嘅老師、同學同朋友。

   You are going back to your country for good. Your classmates hold a farewell party to say goodbye to you. You are expressing your gratitude and thank your teachers, classmates and friends in the party.

7. Listening and speaking

聽説練習 tingsyut lihnjaahp

7.1 In a restaurant

阿王：	噚日我嘅加拿大朋友打電話俾我，請我聖誕節去探佢。	**A Wóng:**	Kàhmyaht ngóhge Gānàhdaaih pàhngyáuh dá dihnwá béi ngóh, chéng ngóh Singdaan jit heui taam kéuih.
安德：	聖誕節嗰陣時，加拿大凍過香港。平時落好多雪，真係好凍，你唔鍾意凍（嘅天氣），不如請佢嚟香港過年啦。	**Ōndāk:**	Sīngdaan jit gójahnsìh, Gānàhdaaih dunggwo Hēunggóng. Pìhngsìh lohk hóudō syut, jānhaih hóudung, néih m̀jūngyi dung (ge tīnhei), bātyùh chéng kéuih làih Hēunggóng gwo nìhn lā.
阿王：	係嘛！如果佢嚟香港過年，我哋又可以行花市又可以一齊攞／掟利是，噉，同喺加拿大過聖誕一樣咁開心。	**A Wóng:**	Haih bo! Yùhgwó kéuih làih Hēunggóng gwonìhn, ngóhdeih yauh hóyíh hàahng fāsíh yauh hóyíh yātchàih ló/dauh laihsih, gám, tùhng hái Gānàhdaaih gwo Singdaan yātyeuhng gam hōisām.

General Review L1-L10

1. ## You are chatting with your friends in a restaurant. Please answer the following questions.

   Fongga gójahnsìh néih jūngyi jouh dī mātyéh a?

   _____

   Néih wúih m̀wúih gaaisiuh pàhngyáuh làih Hēunggóng Jūngmàhn Daaihhohk hohkGwóngdūngwá a? Dímgáai nē?

   _____

   Hái nīdouh hàahng heui fóchējaahm yiu géinoih a?

   _____

   Chéng mahn chóhhái néih jóbihn gógo yàhn haih bīngwok yàhn a?

   _____

   Néih dásyun duhkyùhn Gwóngdūngwá jīhauh jouh mātyéh a?

   _____

   Hēunggóng yáuhdī mātyéh hóu chēutméng ge yéh a?

   _____

   Néih heui Dākgwok gójahnsìh, néih chóh yahttáu dihng yehmáahn ge fēigēi a?

   _____

   Néihge séjihlàuh léuihbihn m̀jí yáuh gīngléih, juhng yáuh mātyéh jīkyùhn a?

   _____

   Yùhgwó néih haih gīngléih, yáuh jīkyùhn tàuhsou néih m̀hóu, néih dím chyúhléih a?

   _____

2. ## Fill in the blanks with appropriate word(s).

   Kàhmyaht Máhlaih tùhng pàhngyáuh heui yámchàh, sihkjó _____ tùhng _____ dángdáng ge dímsām.

   Jēung sīnsāang hóu jūngyi jouh wahnduhng, kéuih jūngyi dá _____ tùhng

_____.

Ngóh gaaisiuh _____ béi _____ sīk.

Ngóh ngūkkéi ge deihjí haih _____

_____.

Chàhn síujé yeukjó ngóh hái _____ chìhnbihn dáng kéuih.

Múihnìhn Chīngmìhngjit tùhng Chùhngyèuhngjit, hóudō Jūnggwok yàhn dōu heui _____ tùhng _____.

A-Mēi hàahngheui Jīmsājéui _____ chóh syùhn heui _____.

Ngóhdeih hóyíh chóh _____ tùhng _____ heui Sāandéng.

Kéuih fāan Jūngdaaih gójahnsìh, m̀jí yiu chóh deihtit, juhng yiu hái Gáulùhngtòhng jyun _____ làih nīdouh.

Hohksāang hóyíh heui yúhyìhn sahtyihmsāt (language laboratory) tēng _____ tùhng dá _____.

3. Texts

課文 fomàhn

3.1 On campus

保羅：	你知唔知李先生幾時生日呀？	Bóulòh:	Néih jīm̀jī Léih sīnsāang géisìh sāangyaht a?
瑪麗：	我知，李先生下個禮拜三（三月十四號）生日，李先生係我哋班嘅先生，我哋買乜嘢禮物俾佢呀？	Máhlaih:	Ngóh jī, Léih sīnsāang hahgo láihbaaisāam (sāamyuhtsahpsei houh) sāangyaht. Léih sīnsāang haih ngóhdeih bāan ge sīnsāang, ngóhdeih máaih mātyéh láihmaht béi kéuih a?
保羅：	我哋買一個好靚嘅錶俾佢，好唔好呀？	Bóulòh:	Ngóhdeih máaih yātgo hóu lengge bīu béi kéuih, hóu m̀hóu a?
王先生：	靚嘅錶太貴，我哋唔夠錢。	Wòhng sīnsāang:	Lengge bīu taai gwai, ngóhdeih m̀gau chín.

瑪麗：	我哋買啲花俾佢，好唔好呀？	**Máhlaih:**	Ngóhdeih máaih dī fā béi kéuih, hóu m̀hóu a?
王先生：	李先生係男人，我知道佢唔鍾意花。	**Wòhng sīnsāang:**	Léih sīnsāang haih nàahmyán, ngóh jīdou kéuihm̀jūngyi fā.
保羅：	我哋買一件新衫俾李先生，好唔好呀？	**Bóulòh:**	Ngóhdeih máaih yātgihn sānsāam béi Léih sīnsāang, hóu m̀hóu a?
瑪麗、王先生：	好好。我哋幾時去買呀？	**Máhlaih, Wòhng sīnsāang:**	Hóu hóu. Ngóhdeih géisìh heui máaih a?
保羅：	今日我哋十一點四放學。我哋去百貨公司買啦。	**Bóulòh:**	Gāmyaht ngóhdeih sahpyātdímsei fonghohk. Ngóhdeih heui baakfo gūngsī máaih lā.
王先生：	下個禮拜三我哋十二點四放學。我哋班嘅同學同李先生去美心酒樓飲茶，好唔好呀？	**Wòhng sīnsāang:**	Hahgo láihbaaisāam ngóhdeih sahpyihdímsei fonghohk. Ngóhdeih bāan ge tùhnghohk tùhng Léih sīnsāang heui Méihsām jáulàuh yámchàh, hóu m̀hóu a?
保羅、瑪麗：	好！去邊間美心酒樓呀？	**Bóulòh, Máhlaih:**	Hóu! Heui bīngāan Méihsām jáulàuh a?
王先生：	去沙田火車站嗰間啦。	**Wòhng sīnsāang:**	Heui Sātìhn fóchējaahm gógāan lā.

Appendices 附錄
Appendix I: Index of pragmatic points 語用點索引

Appendix II: Index of grammatical points 語法點索引

Appendix III: Vocabulary index 活用詞彙總表

Yale Romanization	Chinese characters	Part of speech	English	Lesson number	Page number
a ?	呀？	Part	questioning particle	Lesson 1	5
àh ?!	嘎？！	Part	reconfirming particle	Lesson 1	5
bāan	班	N	class	Lesson 1	5
baahn chīmjing	辦簽證	V	to apply for visa	Lesson 8	113
bātgwo	不過	Adv	however	Lesson 6	87
bātjóyihp	畢咗業	PH	graduated	Lesson 6	88
behngjó	病咗	PH	be sick	Lesson 7	103
béichín	俾錢	V	to pay	Lesson 8	113
béigaau	比較	Adj	comparetinely, relatively	Lesson 6	88
bénggōn	餅乾	N	biscuits	Lesson 7	103
bīn fōngmihn?	邊方面？	PH	which aspect?	Lesson 10	138
bīndī deihfōng	邊啲地方	PH	which places	Lesson 4	53
bīndouh	邊度	QW	where?	Lesson 2	20
bīngwok	邊國	QW	Which country?	Lesson 1	5
bīnyaht	邊日	PH	which date	Lesson 5	68
bōng	幫	V	to help	Lesson 5	69
bōngsáu	幫手	V	to help	Lesson 6	87
būi	杯	N/M	cup	Lesson 3	37
chāmdō	差唔多	Adj	almost the same, similar	Lesson 10	137

cháai dāanchē	踩單車	V	to ride on bicycle	Lesson 10	137
chāamgā	參加	V	to participate in	Lesson 10	138
chāamgūn	參觀	V	to visit a place	Lesson 9	125
chāantēng	餐廳	N	restaurant	Lesson 2	20
chàhlàuh	茶樓	N	tea house	Lesson 7	103
chē pàaih	車牌	N	car licence, car number plate; driving licence	Lesson 9	125
chéng néih sihkfaahn	請你食飯	PH	buy you meal	Lesson 3	37
chìhjó	遲咗	PH	to be late	Lesson 9	126
chìhnbihn	前邊	N	in front	Lesson 2	20
chíngmahn	請問	PH	would like to ask…	Lesson 2	20
chóh	坐	V	to sit, to take vehicle	Lesson 7	103
chóh chē	坐車	V	to ride in a car	Lesson 9	125
chóh syùhn	坐船	V	to take a ferry/boat	Lesson 10	137
chòuh	嘈	Adj	noisy	Lesson 10	137
dá móhngkàuh	打網球	V	to play tennis	Lesson 4	52
daaih	大	Adj	big	Lesson 1	5
daaihgā	大家	N	everyone	Lesson 6	88
daaihkoi	大概	Adv	about, approximately	Lesson 7	104
dábō	打波	V	to play ball	Lesson 4	52
dahkbiht	特別	Adj	special	Lesson 10	137
daih yāt chi	第一次	PH	the first time	Lesson 6	87
dájó jām	打咗針	Ph	injected	Lesson 7	104
dākhàahn	得閒	PH	be free	Lesson 5	69
dáng yāt dáng	等一等	PH	wait for a while	Lesson 5	68
dáng	等	V	to wait	Lesson 3	37

dásyun	打算	V/N	to plan, plan	Lesson 8	112
dehngwái	訂位	V	to make reservation	Lesson 7	103
deihdouh	地道	Adj	with local taste	Lesson 7	102
deihtit	地鐵	N	MTR, subway	Lesson 9	125
deui mjyuh	對唔住	PH	sorry	Lesson 2	20
deui ngóh láih góng taai nàahn	對我嚟講太難	PH	too difficult for me	Lesson 10	137
deuimihn	對面	TW	opposite to	Lesson 7	103
dī	啲	M	some	Lesson 4	53
…dím a?	……點呀？	PH	how is … ?	Lesson 10	137
Dihksih nèih	迪士尼	PW	Disneyland	Lesson 5	68
dihng sìhgaan	定時間	PH	set a time	Lesson 5	69
dihnghaih	定係	Patt	or	Lesson 3	37
dihnyíng	電影	N	movie	Lesson 2	21
dīksí	的士	N	taxi	Lesson 9	125
dímgáai	點解	QW	why	Lesson 7	103
dímjouh	點做	QW	what to do	Lesson 9	126
dímsām	點心	N	dimsum	Lesson 7	102
dímsyun	點算	QW	what can be done	Lesson 9	125
dímyéung	點樣	QW	how	Lesson 7	103
dōdī	多啲	PH	more	Lesson 6	88
dōjeh	多謝	PH	thank you	Lesson 3	37
dou	到	V	to arrive	Lesson 5	69
dōu	都	Adv	also	Lesson 4	52
dou sìh gin	到時見	PH	see you then	Lesson 5	69
duhksyū	讀書	V	to study	Lesson 6	88
dung	凍	Adj	cold	Lesson 3	37
fāanlàih	返嚟	V	to come back	Lesson 6	87

Faatgwok choi	法國菜	N	French cuisine	Lesson 6	87
faatsīu	發燒	V	to have fever	Lesson 7	103
fānjūng	分鐘	N	minute	Lesson 9	125
fēi (jēung)	飛 (張)	N	ticket	Lesson 5	68
fōngbihn	方便	Adj	convenient	Lesson 10	138
fongga	放假	V	to have vacation	Lesson 8	112
fōngheung	方向	N	direction	Lesson 8	113
fuhgahn	附近	TW	nearby	Lesson 7	103
fuhkmouh	服務	N	service	Lesson 7	103
fūnggíng	風景	N	scenary	Lesson 8	113
fūnsung wúi	歡送會	N	farewell party	Lesson 5	69
fūnyìhng gwōnglàhm	歡迎光臨	PH	welcome	Lesson 3	37
gaaisiuh…sīk	介紹…識	V	to introduce	Lesson 1	5
gaau	教	V	to teach	Lesson 3	37
gāautūng	交通	N	transportation	Lesson 10	138
gafē	咖啡	N	coffee	Lesson 3	37
gám	噉	Part	then	Lesson 2	21
gám yéung	噉樣	PH	in this way	Lesson 10	137
gāmmāan / gāmmáahn	今晚	TW	tonight	Lesson 2	21
gámmouh	感冒	N	flu	Lesson 7	104
gāmyaht	今日	TW	today	Lesson 3	37
gau	夠	Adj	enough	Lesson 8	113
gēichèuhng	機場	N	airport	Lesson 6	87
géidím	幾點	PH	what time	Lesson 5	69
géidō chín	幾多錢	PH	How much money	Lesson 4	53
gēipiu	機票	N	air ticket	Lesson 9	126

géisìh	幾時	QW	when?	Lesson 2	21
gewah	嘅話	PH	in case	Lesson 4	53
ginjūk	建築	N	architecture	Lesson 8	113
ginmihn	見面	V	to meet	Lesson 5	69
giu	叫	V	called	Lesson 1	4
gódouh	嗰度	PW	there	Lesson 4	52
gógo	嗰個	SP	that one	Lesson 4	53
gói	改	V	to change, to correct	Lesson 9	126
gokdāk	覺得	V	to feel	Lesson 10	137
gōmóuh bíuyín	歌舞表演	N	singing and dancing show	Lesson 10	137
gón mdóu	趕唔到	PH	cannot catch (vehicle)	Lesson 9	126
góng béi néih jī	講俾你知	PH	tell you	Lesson 5	69
góyaht	嗰日	TW	that day	Lesson 5	69
guih	癐	Adj	tired	Lesson 10	137
gūnghéi	恭喜	V	congratulate	Lesson 10	138
gūngjok	工作	N	work	Lesson 10	138
gūngjok seuhnleih	工作順利	PH	best wishes in work	Lesson 10	138
gwo	過	BF	experienced	Lesson 6	87
gwójāp	果汁	N	fruit juice	Lesson 3	37
Gwóngdūngwá	廣東話	N	Cantonese language	Lesson 1	5
hàahng	行	V	to walk	Lesson 8	113
hàahnggāai	行街	V	to go window shopping	Lesson 4	53
háausíh	考試	N	examination	Lesson 2	21
hahchi	下次	PH	next time	Lesson 6	87

hahjau	下晝	TW	afternoon	Lesson 3	37
hahpsīk	合適	Adj	suitable	Lesson 10	138
hahtīn	夏天	TW	summer	Lesson 8	112
hái	喺	V	to be located	Lesson 2	20
haih	係	V	to be	Lesson 1	4
hauhbihn	後邊	N	behind	Lesson 2	20
héisān	起身	V	to wake up	Lesson 7	103
heui	去	V	to go	Lesson 2	20
Hēunggóng yàhn	香港人	N	Hong Kong people	Lesson 1	5
hīngsūng	輕鬆	Adj	relaxed	Lesson 10	137
hohk	學	V	to learn	Lesson 1	5
hohkhaauh wuhtduhng	學校活動	N	school activities	Lesson 8	112
hohksāang	學生	N	student	Lesson 1	5
hōi	開	V	to open	Lesson 5	69
hóibīn	海邊	PW	sea side	Lesson 3	36
hōichí	開始	V	to start	Lesson 10	138
hōisām	開心	Adj	happy	Lesson 6	87
hólohk	可樂	N	Cola	Lesson 3	37
hóu	好	Adv	very	Lesson 1	5
hóu noih	好耐	Adj	long time	Lesson 10	137
hóu sihk	好食	Adj	good taste	Lesson 4	52
hóu wáan	好玩	Adj	fun	Lesson 10	137
houhmáh	號碼	N	number	Lesson 6	87
hóyíh	可以	AV	can, permitted to, able to	Lesson 5	68
jaahpgwaan	習慣	V/N	be used to; habit	Lesson 10	138
jānhaih	真係	Adv	really	Lesson 9	125

jauhhaih	就係	Adv	that is	Lesson 4	53
jāumuht	周末	TW	weekend	Lesson 3	36
jeui dō	最多	PH	the most	Lesson 9	125
jéunbeih	準備	V	to prepare	Lesson 8	113
jīchìhn	之前	Adv	before	Lesson 5	69
jīdou	知道	V	to know	Lesson 2	20
jíhaih	只係	Adv	only	Lesson 9	125
jīhauh	之後	Adv	after	Lesson 5	69
jihkdāk tái	值得睇	PH	worth-seeing	Lesson 8	112
jihngdī	靜啲	PH	quieter	Lesson 10	137
jihyìhn	自然	N	nature	Lesson 8	113
jingmìhng	證明	V/N	to prove, proof	Lesson 8	113
jip	接	V	to meet and pick up	Lesson 6	87
jóbihn	左邊	N	left	Lesson 2	20
joigin	再見	PH	see you again	Lesson 2	20
jouh wahnduhng	做運動	V	to do sports	Lesson 2	20
jouhyéh	做嘢	V	to work (lit. to do things)	Lesson 10	138
jóusàhn	早晨	PH	Good morning	Lesson 1	5
jóyáu	左右	Adv	approximately	Lesson 7	103
juhng	仲	Adv	still	Lesson 4	52
jūk néih sìhnggūng	祝你成功	PH	wish you success	Lesson 10	138
jūnghohk	中學	N	secondary school	Lesson 6	88
júngleuih	種類	N	type, kind	Lesson 7	103
Jungmahn	中文	N	Chinese language	Lesson 1	5
Jūngmàhn Daaihhohk	中文大學	N	The Chinese University of Hong Kong	Lesson 1	5

Jūngmàhn méng	中文名	N	Chinese name	Lesson 1	5
jūngngh	中午	TW	noon	Lesson 7	103
Jūngwàahn	中環	PW	Central	Lesson 4	53
jūngyi	鍾意	V	to like	Lesson 1	5
jyunjó	轉左	V	to turn left	Lesson 8	113
kāat	卡	N	card	Lesson 5	68
kàhmyaht	噙日	TW	yesterday	Lesson 4	53
kéuih	佢	Pronoun	he, she, him, her	Lesson 1	4
lā	啦	P	sentence particle showing suggestions	Lesson 3	37
làih	嚟	V	to come	Lesson 6	87
làuhhohk sāang	留學生	N	study abroad student	Lesson 6	87
làuhjó hái fóchē seuhngbihn	留咗喺火車上便	PH	left in the train	Lesson 9	125
làuhyìhn	留言	VO	to leave message	Lesson 5	69
lèih	離	Adv	apart	Lesson 7	103
leng	靚	Adj	pretty	Lesson 1	5
lèuhng	涼	Adj	cool	Lesson 8	112
léuihhàhng	旅行	V/N	travel	Lesson 10	137
lihksí	歷史	N	history	Lesson 8	113
lihngngoih	另外	Adv	another, other	Lesson 9	126
ló	攞	V	to take, to bring	Lesson 9	125
lohkchē	落車	V	to take off car	Lesson 9	125
lóuhbáan	老闆	N	boss	Lesson 4	53
louh seuhngbihn	路上便	PH	on the way; on the road	Lesson 10	137
louhháu	路口	N	road junction	Lesson 8	113
lóuhsī	老師	N	teacher	Lesson 1	5

lyùhnlok	聯絡	V	to be in touch (with people)	Lesson 9	126
maahnmáan	慢慢	Adv	slowly; gradually	Lesson 10	137
máaih	買	V	to buy	Lesson 4	53
maaihsaai	賣晒	PH	Sold out	Lesson 3	37
màhfàahn	麻煩	Adj	troublesome	Lesson 8	113
mahn	問	V	to ask	Lesson 8	113
màhngín	文件	N	document	Lesson 8	113
mān	蚊	N	dollar	Lesson 4	53
mātyéh	乜嘢	QW	what	Lesson 1	4
mātyéh dōu sihk	乜嘢都食	PH	can eat anything	Lesson 3	37
mchīngchó	唔清楚	PH	not clear	Lesson 9	126
mcho	唔錯	PH	not bad	Lesson 9	125
mdāk	唔得	PH	not ok	Lesson 2	21
meih	未	Adv	not yet	Lesson 4	52
Méihgwok yàhn	美國人	N	American	Lesson 1	5
méng	名	N	name	Lesson 1	4
mgányiu	唔緊要	PH	never mind, no problem	Lesson 2	20
mgeidāk	唔記得	PH	forgot	Lesson 7	103
mginjó	唔見咗	PH	be missing; to be lost	Lesson 9	125
mgōi	唔該	PH	thank you	Lesson 2	20
mhaih	唔係	PH	not to be	Lesson 1	5
mhóu	唔好	PH	not good	Lesson 4	53
mihnbāau	麵包	N	bread	Lesson 7	103
mihngbaahk	明白	V	to understand	Lesson 9	126
mòhng	忙	Adj	busy	Lesson 6	88

móhngkàuh chèuhng	網球場	PW/N	tennis court	Lesson 4	53
móuh	冇	V	not to have	Lesson 1	5
móuh mahntàih	冇問題	PH	No problem	Lesson 2	21
msái	唔使	PH	no need	Lesson 9	125
msái haakhei	唔使客氣	PH	not at all, don't be polite	Lesson 6	87
msyūfuhk	唔舒服	PH	not feeling well	Lesson 7	103
mtùhng	唔同	Adj	different	Lesson 10	137
nàahm bouh	南部	N	southern part	Lesson 8	113
nám	諗	V	to think	Lesson 7	103
nē ?	呢？	Part	how about?	Lesson 1	5
néihhóu	你好	PH	How are you?	Lesson 1	4
néihdeih	你地	N	you (plural)	Lesson 2	20
ngàhnbāau	銀包	N	purse	Lesson 9	125
ngàuhyuhk sāammàhnjih	牛肉三文治	N	beef sandwiches	Lesson 3	37
ngóh	我	Pronoun	I, me, my	Lesson 1	4
nībāan fēigēi	呢班飛機	PH	this airplane	Lesson 9	126
nīchi	呢次	PH	this time	Lesson 6	87
nīdouh	呢度	PW	here	Lesson 2	20
nīgo	呢個	SP	this one	Lesson 3	36
pàhngyáuh	朋友	N	friend	Lesson 6	87
pèhng	平	Adj	cheap	Lesson 4	52
pèhngdī	平啲	PH	cheaper	Lesson 4	53
pòhngbīn	旁邊	N	next to, beside	Lesson 2	20
pùih	陪	V	to accompany	Lesson 9	125
sāam nìhn chìhn	三年前	PH	three years ago	Lesson 8	112

sāangyaht	生日	V	birthday	Lesson 3	37
Sāangyaht faailohk	生日快樂	PH	Happy birthday	Lesson 3	37
sāileih	犀利	Adj	serious	Lesson 7	104
sān làih ge	新嚟嘅	PH	newly come	Lesson 6	87
sāp	濕	Adj	wet; humid	Lesson 10	138
sáugēi	手機	N	mobile phone	Lesson 6	87
sāugeui	收據	N	receipt	Lesson 9	125
sei dím bun	四點半	PH	half past four	Lesson 5	69
seuhngbihn	上邊	N	on top	Lesson 2	20
seuhngjau	上晝	TW	before noon	Lesson 3	37
séuhngtòhng	上堂	V	to go to class	Lesson 2	20
séung	想	AV	want to	Lesson 2	20
sēungchèuhng	商場	N	shopping mall	Lesson 4	53
seunyuhng kāat (jēung)	信用卡（張）	N	credit card	Lesson 5	68
si	試	V	to try	Lesson 7	102
sìhgaan	時間	N	time	Lesson 3	37
sihkfaahn	食飯	V	to have meal	Lesson 2	20
sihkjó	食咗	PH	have eaten	Lesson 4	52
sing	姓	V	to have surname called	Lesson 1	5
sīngkèih géi	星期幾	PH	which day of the week	Lesson 5	69
sīngkèih sei	星期四	TW	Thursday	Lesson 5	68
síusíu	少少	PH	a little bit	Lesson 6	88
sūkse	宿舍	N	dormitory	Lesson 6	88
sung	送	V	to send	Lesson 7	104

syúnjaahk	選擇	V/N	to choose, choice	Lesson 10	138
taai gwai	太貴	PH	too expensive	Lesson 4	53
tái yīsāng	睇醫生	V	to see doctor	Lesson 7	103
táidóu	睇到	PH	saw, can be seen	Lesson 8	113
táihei	睇戲	V	to watch movie	Lesson 2	21
táiyuhk gún	體育館	PW/N	gymnasium	Lesson 4	53
tānnàh yú sāammàhnjih	吞拿魚三文治	N	tuna fish sandwiches	Lesson 3	37
tàuhtung	頭痛	N	headache	Lesson 7	103
tēnggóng	聽講	PH	I heard that…	Lesson 2	21
teuichín	退錢	V	to refund	Lesson 9	126
tìhnbíu	填表	V	to fill in form	Lesson 8	113
tīngmáahn	聽晚	TW	tomorrow night	Lesson 2	21
tīngyaht gin	聽日見	PH	see you tomorrow	Lesson 2	20
tóuh	肚	N	belly	Lesson 7	103
tùhng pàhngyáuh kīnggái	同朋友傾偈	PH	to chat with friends	Lesson 6	88
ūkkéi	屋企	PW/N	home	Lesson 5	68
waahkjé	或者	Adv	or, maybe	Lesson 7	103
waahkwá	畫畫	V	to draw, to paint	Lesson 6	88
wàahngíng	環境	N	environment	Lesson 9	125
wáanháh	玩下	PH	to have fun	Lesson 3	36
wàhkìuh	華僑	N	Overseas Chinese	Lesson 1	5
waihtung	胃痛	N	stomach ache	Lesson 7	104
wán	搵	V	to find; to look for	Lesson 4	53
wán yéh jouh	搵嘢做	PH	find job (lit. find things to do)	Lesson 10	138
wánfāan	搵返	PH	found, to be found	Lesson 9	126

wānjaahp	溫習	V	to review, to study	Lesson 2	21
yahpjó yīyún	入咗醫院	PH	to be hospitalized	Lesson 7	103
yám	飲	V	to drink	Lesson 3	37
yámchàh	飲茶	V	to have dimsum (lit. to drink tea)	Lesson 3	37
yātchàih	一齊	Adv	together	Lesson 4	52
yātdihng	一定	Adv	definitely	Lesson 10	138
yātguhng	一共	Adv	in total	Lesson 5	68
yātjahn(gāan)	一陣（間）	PH	a while	Lesson 1	5
yáuh	有	V	to have	Lesson 1	5
yáuh gēiwuih	有機會	PH	have chance	Lesson 6	87
yáuhdī	有啲	Adv	a little bit	Lesson 10	137
yàuhhaak	遊客	N	tourist	Lesson 10	137
yàuhséui	游水	V	to swim	Lesson 6	87
yāusīk	休息	V	to rest	Lesson 6	88
yāuwaih	優惠	N	discount	Lesson 5	68
yéh	嘢	N	things	Lesson 4	53
yeuhk	藥	N	medicine	Lesson 7	104
yeuk	約	V	to make appointment	Lesson 6	87
yih yuht luhk houh	二月六號	PH	6th February	Lesson 5	68
yìhché	而且	Adv	furthermore	Lesson 7	103
yìhgā	而家	TW	now	Lesson 4	52
yíhhauh	以後	Adv	afterwards	Lesson 6	88
yìhnhauh	然後	Adv	then, afterwards	Lesson 8	112
yihngsīk	認識	V	to know someone	Lesson 6	87
yiht	熱	Adj	hot	Lesson 3	37
yihtnaauh	熱鬧	Adj	bustling	Lesson 10	138

yīnggōi	應該	AV	should	Lesson 9	126
Yīngmàhn	英文	V	English language	Lesson 1	5
yíngséung	影相	V	to take photograph	Lesson 8	113
yiu	要	AV/V	have to, to need	Lesson 2	21
yùhgwó	如果	Adv	if	Lesson 10	138
yúhn	遠	Adj	far	Lesson 7	103
yùhn	完	BF	finish	Lesson 4	52
yuhng	用	V	to use	Lesson 5	68

Appendix IV: Lesson texts in Standard Written Chinese 課文（書面語版）

Lesson 1

In the classroom

老師：	你好！
大衛：	你好！
老師：	你叫甚麼名字？
大衛：	我叫大衛。
老師：	你好，大衛。我是李老師。
大衛：	李老師，你好！
老師：	大家好，我姓李，是你們的老師。
學生：	李老師，你好。

On the campus

子安：	你好！我叫林子安。
大衛：	你好！我叫大衛。
子安：	大衛，你是不是美國人？
大衛：	我是美國華僑。你呢？
子安：	我是香港人。
大衛：	你是不是中文大學學生？
子安：	是，我是中文大學學生。

大衛：	你是中文大學學生？
子安：	是的。你呢？
大衛：	我都是中文大學學生，中文大學很大。
子安：	對！中文大學很大，很美！大衛，你學甚麼？
大衛：	我學中文，我學廣東話，我喜歡中文。你呢？
子安：	我學英文。

In the classroom

大衛：	早晨，這個是不是廣東話班？
老師：	是的。
大衛：	你是不是老師？
老師：	是的，我是廣東話老師，我姓李。
大衛：	李老師，你好！
老師：	你叫甚麼名字？
大衛：	我叫 David White。
老師：	你有沒有中文名？
大衛：	有，我中文名叫白大衛。
老師：	大衛，你是哪國人呢？
大衛：	我是美國人，我是美國華僑。
老師：	你有十六個同學，一會給你介紹。
大衛：	好的！

Lesson 2

On school campus

子安：	大衛、安娜，你們去哪裏？
安娜：	我去上課。

大衛：	我去做運動，你呢？
子安：	我去餐廳食飯。明天見。
大衛：	明天見。
安娜：	再見。

Near the train station

子安：	請問，大學站是不是在前邊？
路人A：	是的，（大學車站）就在前邊。
子安：	謝謝。你知不知道超級市場在哪裏呢？
路人A：	知道，在山上邊，在餐廳旁邊。
子安：	這裏有沒有廁所呢？
路人A：	對不起，我不知（道）。
子安：	不要緊。
大衛：	你知道博物館在哪裏嗎？
路人B：	知道，在辦公大樓左邊。
路人C：	不對，在圖書館後邊。
路人D：	都不對，博物館在火車站後邊。

In the dormitory

大衛：	小文，想去看電影嗎？聽說這部電影很好看。
小文：	好的，你想甚麼時候去呢？
大衛：	今天晚上，好嗎？
小文：	今天晚上不可以。明天有考試，我要複習。
大衛：	那麼，明天晚上呢？
小文：	明天晚上沒問題。
大衛：	好，就明晚去。
小文：	好，明天見。

Lesson 3

In the dormitory

子安：	周末你想做甚麼呢？
安娜：	我想去海邊玩玩。你去不去？
子安：	這個周末我要教英文。
安娜：	那麼，我們明天去吧。明天你有沒有時間呢？
子安：	我明天上午考試，下午有時間。
安娜：	好的，我們明天下午去吧。

On school campus

阿美：	今天是大衛的生日。
子安：	大衛，生日快樂，我請你吃飯。
大衛：	好。謝謝你。
子安：	你想吃甚麼呢？
大衛：	我甚麼都吃。
子安：	那麼，我們去喝茶吃點心吧。

In the canteen

店員：	歡迎光臨，請問想吃些甚麼？
顧客：	我想要四份吞拿魚三文治。
店員：	對不起，吞拿魚三文治賣完了。
顧客：	那麼，我要牛肉三文治吧。
店員：	好，想喝甚麼？要可樂、果汁還是咖啡？
顧客：	要兩杯可樂和兩杯咖啡。
店員：	咖啡，要冷的還是熱的？
顧客：	要熱的。
店員：	好的，請你等一會。

Lesson 4

In the classroom

子安：	大衛，吃過飯沒有？
大衛：	還未 (吃)，現在去吃，你呢？
子安：	我都還未吃。
大衛：	一起去吃吧。(你) 想去哪裏吃呢？
子安：	去車站旁邊那餐廳吧，那裏又便宜又好吃。
大衛：	吃完飯，我們去打球，好不好？
子安：	好。

On school campus

阿王：	大衛呢？
小文：	他跟子安去了打網球。
阿王：	你知道他們在哪裏打球嗎？
小文：	在體育館旁邊的網球場。
阿王：	好，謝謝你，我現在就去那邊找他。

In the classroom

大衛：	小文，昨天你們有沒有打球呢？
小文：	昨天天氣不好，所以沒有打，我們去了逛街。
大衛：	去了哪些地方呢？
小文：	去了中環的商場。
大衛：	買了甚麼呢？
小文：	沒買東西，那裏東西太貴了。

In a shop

阿美：	老闆，這個多少錢呢？
老闆：	這個 29 元。
阿美：	那個呢？
老闆：	哪個？
阿美：	就是上面那個。
老闆：	那個，20 元。
阿美：	我要那個，便宜點，可以嗎？
老闆：	買兩個的話，38 元。
阿美：	好，我要兩個。

Lesson 5

At the ticket office of a theme park

大衛：	請問迪士尼的門票多少錢呢？
售票員：	一張 550 元。你要多少張呢？
大衛：	我要兩張。學生有沒有優惠呢？
售票員：	沒有的，學生沒有優惠。一共 1100 元。
大衛：	可以用信用卡嗎？
售票員：	可以。
大衛：	好，請你等一等。這張是我的信用卡。

In the classroom

安娜：	子安，我們哪天去小文家呢？
子安：	二月六日，星期四。
安娜：	那日我有考試。
子安：	你幾點考完試？

安娜：	四點三十分。
子安：	那麼，沒問題，我們六點之前到他家就可以了。
安娜：	我們在哪裏等呢？
子安：	在大學圖書館前面等，好嗎？
安娜：	好，我們幾點見面呢？
子安：	下午六點，可以嗎？
安娜：	好，到時見。

Over the phone

小文：	喂，安娜，我是小文。
安娜：	你好，小文。
小文：	我們想為你們開一個歡送會，我想知道你星期幾有空？
安娜：	我星期一到星期三晚都有空。
小文：	好，我們定了時間之後，再告訴你吧。
安娜：	好。謝謝你。

小文打電話給子安約他去歡送會

子安：	你好，我沒空聽電話。請你在 "啲" 一聲之後留言。
小文：	我們幫安娜開一個歡送會，我想知道你下星期三有沒有時間。你有空就打電話給我吧。謝謝。

Lesson 6

On school campus

安德：	你好。我叫安德，我是新來的留學生。
阿王：	你好。我叫王子強 Aaron，朋友們都叫我，阿王。
安德：	阿王，很高興認識你。
阿王：	我都很開心。這次是不是你第一次來香港呢？

安德：	是的，我以前沒有來過香港。
阿王：	那麼，有甚麼要幫忙，就找我，不用客氣。我的手機號碼是 9876543。
安德：	謝謝你。我還未有香港的手機號碼。有的話，我就告訴你吧。

In the dormitory

阿王：	我回來了。
安德：	阿王，你今天不用上課？
阿王：	今天沒課。一會我要去機場接我媽媽。
安德：	她從哪裏來呢？
阿王：	她從波爾多來。
安德：	波爾多在哪裏？
阿王：	在法國，你知道法國在哪裏嗎？
安德：	知道，我吃過法國菜，法國菜很貴。
阿王：	你喜歡吃嗎？
安德：	很喜歡。
阿王：	那麼，今天晚上，我們一起去吃法國菜，好嗎？
安德：	好，不過今晚我約了朋友。
阿王：	不要緊，下次有機會再一起吃吧。
安德：	好。

In the dormitory

安德：	阿王，你有空的時候，喜歡做甚麼呢？
阿王：	我喜歡打球和游泳。
安德：	在德國，我會去公園畫畫，跟朋友聊天。來了香港之後，學習比較忙，有空時，就在宿舍休息。我現在最喜歡學中文。
阿王：	那就好，我們以後就多用中文聊天吧。

In a restaurant

子安：	大家好，我來介紹一下，這個是我的德國朋友安德。他會説一點點廣東話，請你們多用中文跟他聊天。
安德：	你們好，我叫安德。很高興認識你們。
嘉欣：	安德，你好。我叫嘉欣，我是子安的中學同學。
安德：	你好。你現在還是學生嗎？
嘉欣：	我已經畢業了，現在在一間美國 IT 公司工作。你呢？
安德：	我是留學生，現在在中文大學，學國際商業。

Lesson 7

In the classroom

安娜：	這次是我第一次來香港，一定要試一試廣東點心。
安德：	我去過一間很地道的茶樓，叫明星茶樓。
安娜：	那裏的點心，種類多不多？
安德：	種類很多，而且都很好吃，還有，他們的服務都很好。
安娜：	貴不貴呢？
安德：	我忘了，一個人大概一百元吧。
安娜：	那間茶樓在哪裏呢？離這裏遠不遠呢？
安德：	不遠。
安娜：	在這裏怎樣去呢？
安德：	在這裏，坐火車去，坐兩個站，就到了。

Over the phone

安德：	喂，德華，我是安德。
德華：	安德，你好。找我有甚麼事呢？
安德：	明天中午有沒有時間呢？我和嘉欣想約你和德寶吃飯。

德華：	很好，在哪裏吃呢？
安德：	我們想去明星茶樓。你知道在哪裏嗎？
德華：	我想我知道，是不是在九龍公園附近呢？
安德：	是的，就在九龍公園對面。
德華：	好，知道了。明天中午幾點呢？
安德：	中午十二點三十分，可以嗎？
德華：	好，沒問題。訂了位沒有呢？
安德：	已經訂了，訂了安先生，四位。
德華：	好。明天見。

In the dormitory

阿王：	安德，你為甚麼還不起床呢？是不是不舒服？
安德：	是的，我想我病了。
阿王：	你哪裏不舒服呢？
安德：	頭痛，我覺得我發燒。肚子都有點不舒服。
阿王：	你想去看醫生嗎？
安德：	我現在不想去，我想休息一下。
阿王：	好，那，你休息一會，我先去上課。
安德：	你回來的時候，可不可以幫幫我，你可不可以買些東西給我吃呢？
阿王：	沒問題，你想吃甚麼呢？
安德：	餅乾或者麵包都可以。

Over the phone

德華：	安德，你現在在哪裏？
安德：	我現在在家休息。
德華：	聽說你昨天入了醫院，你怎麼啦？
安德：	我沒留院，不過我在醫院急症室等了一晚。

德華：	甚麼事？
安德：	前晚我忽然胃痛，痛得很利害，所以就去醫院急症室。
德華：	你怎樣去醫院的？
安德：	我的朋友送我去。
德華：	那麼，你知道為甚麼胃痛呢？
安德：	醫生説可能是感冒，護士幫我打針，還給我些藥，之後就叫我回家了。
德華：	那麼，你為甚麼在醫院等了一晚呢？
安德：	因病人太多，所以我在那裏等了很長時間。

Lesson 8

In the dormitory

安德：	阿王，放假的時候，你有甚麼打算呢？
阿王：	七月，我會去英國。
安德：	去英國哪裏呢？
阿王：	去倫敦，參加一個學校活動，然後在那裏玩幾天。
安德：	我三年前去過倫敦。夏天去倫敦不錯，夏天倫敦天氣比香港涼快很多。
阿王：	我知道倫敦有很多值得看的歷史建築。
安德：	對呀。如果你喜歡自然風景，還可以去南部海岸玩玩。
阿王：	我甚麼地方都想去，不過還要看我的錢夠不夠。對，我明天要去辦簽證。
安德：	辦簽證麻煩嗎？
阿王：	很麻煩，要填表，拍照，也要準備證明文件，而且要付錢。

On the street

安德：	對不起，我想問問，世界大樓是不是在附近呢？
路人：	是的，距離這裏不遠，就在前面，你看到展覽中心嗎？
安德：	看到。

路人：	你朝那個方向行，過了前面那個路口，向左拐，就看到了。
安德：	謝謝。

Lesson 9

On school campus

安德：	正風，你好。歡迎你來我們的學校參觀。
劉正風：	謝謝你來接我。你們學校距離市區不是太遠。
安德：	對呀，從中環坐地鐵過來，只要四十五分鐘。
劉正風：	你的宿舍在哪裏呢？
安德：	在山上面，行上去，會很累，我們坐車上去吧。
劉正風：	幾點有車呢？
安德：	三點三十分有車，我們在這裏等等吧。
劉正風：	要買票嗎？
安德：	不用。
劉正風：	這裏的環境真不錯。哎呀！
安德：	甚麼事呢？
劉正風：	我的錢包不見了。怎麼辦？
安德：	是不是留在火車上面呢？
劉正風：	我都不知道。
安德：	我陪你去火車站問一問吧。

In a shopping mall

安德：	我們想先去火車站接朋友，之後去參觀博物館。
劉正風：	那麼，你們坐的士去火車站吧。
安德：	坐的士去，大概要多少錢呢？
劉正風：	最多三十元。下車時要拿收據。

安德：	收據是甚麼？為甚麼要拿收據呢？
劉正風：	收據上面有的士的車牌號碼，如果你在車上面掉了東西……
安德：	明白，有這個號碼，我們就可以找到這輛車。
劉正風：	對呀，那就可以幫你把東西找回來。

At the airport

安德：	對不起，麻煩你幫一幫我。
職員：	有甚麼事呢？
安德：	我坐的火車遲了，現在趕不到這班飛機。我應該怎樣做呢？
職員：	讓我看一看你的機票。這類機票不可以改期。
安德：	你的意思是我不可以改坐下一班機。
職員：	對，你要另外買一張機票。
安德：	那麼，我這張機票可不可以退錢呢？
職員：	那麼，我就不清楚了。你要聯絡客戶服務中心。
安德：	好。那，下班機有沒有位子呢？
職員：	還有。

Lesson 10

In the classroom

德華：	這次旅行怎麼樣呢？
安德：	非常好。桂林山水好特別，跟我見過的很不同。
德華：	你們有沒有去陽朔呢？
安德：	去了，我們在桂林坐船去。
德華：	聽說那裏的風景比桂林更美。你覺得是不是呢？
安德：	我覺得兩個地方的風景差不多，不過陽朔安靜些，桂林的遊客太多，有些嘈吵。
德華：	那裏地方很大，要不要走很久呢？累不累？

安德：	我們騎自行車，一面騎自行車一面看風景，又輕鬆又好玩。
德華：	騎自行車，對我太難了。我騎得不好。
安德：	在那裏，路上車不多，慢慢騎就可以。
德華：	除了看風景，你們在那裏，還做了些甚麼呢？
安德：	我們在那裏還看了一個歌舞表演。
德華：	值得看嗎？
安德：	值得呀，我從來都沒有看過這樣的歌舞表演。
德華：	如果有時間，我都想去。
安德：	如果你沒有去過，就一定要去一次。

On school campus

子安：	安德，時間過得很快，你下星期就要回德國了。
安德：	對呀，時間過得太快了。
子安：	我記得你來的時候不是太喜歡香港。
安德：	對呀，我六月來，那時天氣又熱又潮濕，真的不習慣。
子安：	現在習慣了沒有呢？
安德：	我現在都還未習慣香港的夏天，不過我越來越喜歡香港。
子安：	你喜歡香港哪方面呢？
安德：	我喜歡香港，交通方便，很熱鬧，在外邊吃飯，選擇很多，不是太貴。
子安：	那麼，你想在香港找工作嗎？
安德：	如果有機會，我會試一下。

In the farewell party

安德：	小文，謝謝你來參加這個歡送會。
小文：	我很開心見到你。聽說你很快就要回德國了。
安德：	對呀，我下個月開始工作了。
小文：	嘩，已經找到工作了，恭喜你。是回德國工作嗎？

安德：	不是，是在美國紐約。你呢？畢業之後，有甚麼打算呢？
小文：	我正在找工作，希望找到合適的工作。
安德：	祝你成功！
小文：	謝謝你，我也祝你工作順利。